PRAISE FOR
THE GRIM GRUESOME BOOKS

"amusing...dramatic...just the thing for...readers...who want Dahl-style jokes and adventure." - *The Times*

"smashing...a real adventure story...horrible but also funny... A wonderful book" - *TES Connect*

"...the tales rattle along with great energy and fun... these books will be well loved by many children, who will wait impatiently for the next in the series."
- *School Librarian*

"All the frosty bearded splendour of the Norse sagas condensed into a fun, thrilling tale for kids with a taste for high adventure...tipped to be a best-selling series." - *www.waterstones.com (5-star bookseller review)*

"full of twists and turns that you are desperate to follow." *-www.writeaway.org.uk*

"An outstanding novel, keeping you tense and on edge." - *Imogen, 10*
"adventurous, exciting, action-packed!" - *Uji, 11*
"gripping" - *Ben, 8*   "truly thrilling" - *Megan, 10*
"brilliant...I kept wanting to read the next chapter"-
Adam, 8   - Members of York Children's Book Group

GRIM GRUESOME
VIKING VILLAIN

in

TROLLS' TREASURE

ROSALIND KERVEN

www.grimgruesome.com

A big thank you to my fantastic publishing team:
Editor: Helen Greathead
Designer: Alison Gadsby
Artist: David Wyatt

First published in the UK by Talking Stone 2010

Text copyright © Rosalind Kerven 2010
Illustrations copyright © David Wyatt 2008, 2010

Talking Stone
an author-led publishing team
Swindonburn Cottage West, Sharperton
Morpeth, Northumberland, NE65 7AP

ISBN: 978-0-9537454-5-6

Collect the whole series of books about

GRIM GRUESOME
Viking Villain:

THE CURSED SWORD

Shortlisted for the Solihull Children's Book Award 2009

THE QUEEN'S POISON

Longlisted for the Lancashire Fantastic Book Award 2010

TROLLS' TREASURE

coming soon:
THE RINGS OF DOOM

visit
www.grimgruesome.com
to find out more!

THE NORTH LANDS
A THOUSAND YEARS AGO
THE VIKING AGE

Come back through time to
the Viking realm of Orkney!

Orkney was a scatter of rich, green islands
in the grey sea north of Scotland,
dotted with farms and
mysterious, grass-covered mounds.
It was ruled by a fierce jarl
who piled his feasting tables with beef and cream.
Few trees grew on the islands,
but great birds soared on the endless wind
and the air shimmered with rainbows.

SHETLAND

TROLL-MOUND

BIRD ISLAND

MUDDY BAY

FORTRESS ISLAND

MAINLAND

TIDE POINT

EBB BAY

HIGH ISLAND

ORKNEY

SCOTLAND

1

It was Midsummer Morning. A thick mist hung over the south shore of Mainland, Orkney's largest island.

Some farm boys were wandering along the beach, collecting edible seaweed.

'Look!' one of them yelled suddenly. 'Across the bay there on the rocks – there's a stranded seal!'

They all turned to stare. It was actually a seal *pup*, only a few days old. Its pure white fur stood out starkly against the flat, dark rocks.

The boys started jumping up and down, yelling with excitement.

'Dwarf spit! Look at its fantastic fur!'

'Come on, let's skin it. It'll be worth a fortune!'

'Ya, and we can sell its meat too.'

'Let's kill it now!'

'Ya, club it to death!'

'We'll need heavy sticks…'

'We've got loads on our farm. Come on, let's get them.'

'But supposing the seal escapes while we're gone?'

'Someone guard it.'

They all hesitated…then looked at a tall, stocky lad with frayed trousers and lots of patches on his tunic.

'Ragi can do that.'

'But can we trust him?'

They jostled around Ragi, waving their fists at him.

'This seal's really valuable, understand?'

'Don't you dare let it get away!'

Ragi nodded.

The other lads ran off to the fields above the shore, leapfrogged over a wooden fence and headed for some stone farm buildings in the distance.

Ragi watched them go. He made sure the boys were out of sight, then ran round the bay. At the far end, he clambered quickly over the rocks towards the seal pup.

It watched him with huge, liquid eyes, twitching fearfully.

Ragi went right up to it. He squatted down and

pushed his arms underneath the pup. Its fur was damp and it had a milky, fishy smell. Ragi took firm hold of it and straightened up, groaning under its blubbery weight. Lucky he was really strong! The seal pup wriggled hopelessly and snarled at him like a dog. It beat its flippers wildly, almost catching Ragi in the eye.

Ragi flinched. He gritted his teeth and staggered to the edge of the rocks. There he lowered the pup gently into the sea.

'Swim, friend,' he whispered. 'Go. Quickly!'

As soon as it touched the water, the seal pup was transformed. It turned to face the mouth of the bay and dived vigorously away.

Just in time! For at that moment, a racket of voices yelled:

'YOU STUPID, USELESS, SLIMY EEL!'

'IDIOT, IDIOT!'

'WHAT IN THOR'S NAME ARE YOU DOING?'

Ragi spun round. The other lads were back – and they were brandishing vicious-looking sticks and clubs.

'Where's the seal, Ragi?'

'Where do you think? The pea-brained clod's gone and chucked it away!'

'Our fortune – gone!'

The boys stomped furiously towards him.

'We told you to *guard* it! Get it back, Ragi!'

'Ya, go on, dive in. You're a good swimmer. Go and catch it!'

Ragi faced them stubbornly, but didn't answer. Several of the lads raised their sticks.

'Get him!' someone shouted.

They surged forward. 'COWARD, COWARD!' they yelled.

Ragi lunged at the smallest boy, wrenched the stick from his hand and gripped it like a sword. As the others came at him, he beat them off fiercely, one by one. Despite his rags, he was as strong and fast as a real warrior.

But there were far too many of them. Ragi didn't stand a chance.

He pelted up the sand onto the grass. But the other boys blocked his way, jeering and threatening him. Ragi dodged, raced down the beach, kicked off his shoes and plunged into the sea.

2

A few of the other lads tried to swim after him. But Ragi was much faster than any of them. They soon gave up and turned back.

Ragi headed on blindly through the waves. At last he stopped and trod water, gasping for breath.

Peering through the swirling mist, he saw that he was in a narrow strip of sea between the headland, and a small islet that sheltered the bay from The Deeps.

Suddenly a large rowing boat loomed out of the murk. Like all Viking boats, it sat low in the water, finely shaped into elegant points at both ends. There was only one man in it – and a horse.

The horse was as dark as midnight. Its mane and tail shimmered damply in the mist like wet silver. The man was heavily wrapped up against the biting

Orkney wind. He wore a billowing cloak, a huge fur hat with a very wide brim and several fur mufflers round his neck and face.

He brought the boat carefully alongside Ragi and leaned over the side.

'Enjoying your swim?' he called. His voice was deep and grating.

Ragi stared up at him. The man's face was lost in the shadows of his mufflers and outsized hat.

'No, I'm not,' he answered. 'It's freezing!' Sure enough, Ragi's lips were turning blue. 'Can I come aboard?'

The man shook his head. 'I like seeing you down there,' he rasped. He let out a honking snort of laughter. 'It's funny! Heh-ha!'

Thor's thunderbolts! thought Ragi. *He's a simpleton! Just my luck!*

'Please help me,' he begged. Water streamed from his straggly hair and down his face. 'The other lads are after me – they want to beat me up!' His teeth were chattering.

The man gave his idiotic, goose-like laugh again. But it seemed he was beginning to understand. He reached over the low side with powerful, hairy hands, grabbed Ragi under his armpits and hauled him in.

Ragi squatted in the bottom, dripping and shivering as the shallow boat rocked on the waves.

3

The man shifted back onto the front bench and took up the oars. He turned the boat skillfully and started rowing away through the Deeps.

There wasn't much room in the little boat, because of the horse. The man really stank of rotten meat. To get away from him, Ragi squatted down and wriggled through the horse's legs. Then he perched awkwardly on the back of the boat. His clothes were sopping wet and he couldn't stop shivering.

'What's your name?' asked the man.

Ragi told him. 'What's yours?'

'Me?' rasped the man. 'I've forgotten. Ya, it's true!'

He pointed to the top of his head – or rather, his fur hat.

'You won't believe this, Ragi, but a couple of years

ago I was a great warrior, living in the court of a very powerful lord! But I got my brains bashed out in a fight. And ever since then I've been…you know, peculiar. Heh-heh-heh!'

The boat rocked alarmingly.

'No more battles for me, laddie,' he said. 'I have to earn my living the fool's way now, by travelling from pillar to post and selling things. I've got nothing left from my former life – except my faithful horse. I depend on him, now I'm just a humble pedlar.'

Ragi nodded. 'Where are you going?' he asked.

'Tide Point,' said the pedlar. 'I'm new in Orkney and don't really know my way around, but I've been told I'll find some good customers there.' He pointed behind him to some bulging leather bags. 'That's my stock of fancy goods to sell. So! You know all about me now. It's your turn to answer *my* questions. Why do those other lads want to beat you up?'

Ragi shook his head.

The pedlar pulled steadily at the oars. 'Aw, you can speak freely with a harmless fool like me. Whatever you say will just go in one ear and straight out the other! And even if I wanted to give away your secrets, no one would believe me. You know what Odin

19

All-Father said: *Be on your guard – but not too much.* And: *It's safe to tell a secret to one man.'*

Suddenly they emerged from the mist. Islands rose from the sea on every side. The horse tossed its head and whinnied. A wind blew up, making Ragi's wet clothes flap about. He really didn't want to answer.

But the foolish pedlar kept on and on at him: 'Tell me, tell me! I'm dying to know. If you trust me, I'll help you.'

In the end Ragi couldn't think of a good excuse to stay silent. So he explained how he'd freed the seal cub, and how the other lads were furious because it was so valuable.

'Ha, ha!' rasped the pedlar. 'That ruined their plans, eh? No wonder they came after you! What ever made you do it?

'It's just that I… You see, I can't kill seals,' said Ragi. 'Or let other folk kill them either.'

'Woah, that must be tricky, living in islands that are swamped with the beasts,' said the pedlar. 'Why not?'

'It's…a family secret,' said Ragi.

'Even more intriguing,' said the pedlar. 'A *dark* secret, eh? Well, you can't shock me. Besides, friends should always speak openly together. I tell you what, let's strike a bargain. You tell me what your secret is. Then I'll tell you a secret of my own. And I swear by Odin, you won't be sorry to hear it!'

4

Ragi shook his head.

'Oh, go on,' the pedlar coaxed him. 'I'm on your side. I want to help you. But I can't unless you tell me why you're in trouble.'

Ragi peered through the horse's legs at the pedlar. All that showed of the man's face between the high fur mufflers and the low fur hat was a dark, ragged beard and a glint of eyes.

The pedlar turned to the horse. 'This boy's as stupid as I am if he doesn't want to hear *my* wonderful secret,' he said.

The horse whinnied softly and nuzzled him. It swished its tail against Ragi's face.

Ragi couldn't help being curious. Before he could stop himself, he was pointing to his bare feet and saying,

'It's just that...well, I've got these...peculiar pieces of skin between my toes. Sort of...webs. Like...you know...' He swallowed and lowered his voice. 'Like on a seal's flippers.'

'Aw Ragi, that's fantastic!' cried the pedlar. 'I heard rumours about people like that before I came to these islands, but I never guessed that you were one. That makes me even more pleased to meet you.'

'Really?' said Ragi doubtfully. 'Most people who find out are horrified.'

'Why?' said the pedlar.

'Because...well, they say I'm not...normal,' said Ragi wretchedly. 'And that it's because my mam's done something wicked. You see, my pa died of sickness a few years ago. And as soon as he was buried, all my uncles accused Mam of poisoning him. They said my webbed feet showed that I wasn't really Pa's son after all – and that my real father must be a finman!'

'What's a finman?' said the pedlar.

Ragi blushed. 'A...a...sea-sorcerer. The type that can shape-shift into a seal.'

The pedlar let out a long breath. 'Shape-shifting! Finmen, seals...you. You're all the same kind, eh? Astonishing! That's nearly as good as *my* secret, lad.'

23

'It's not good; it's horrible,' said Ragi gloomily. 'Mam swears by mighty Thor and Odin All-Father that it's not true. She's never even seen a finman! She doesn't even believe they exist! But my uncles turned my aunts and cousins against us too, and they threw us off the family farm. So now everyone despises us and we're really poor. We live all on our own, in a horrible, tumbledown cottage with only one cow and hardly enough to eat.'

'But if it's just lies, why are you bothered about killing seals?' said the pedlar.

Ragi leaned forward, letting the wind dry the seat of his trousers. He wriggled his webbed toes.

'I suppose...I half wish it *was* true,' he said. 'People are all so horrible to me and Mam, sometimes I pretend that the seals are my real relations and friends. So if I killed one, it would feel like murder.'

'I see,' said the pedlar.

'Dwarf spit! I wish I hadn't told you now,' said Ragi.

'Well, I'm glad you did,' said the pedlar. 'That's the most interesting thing I heard since I got my brains bashed in. And you'll be glad too, when I tell you *my* secret. Because I can help you. And you can help me in return. And we'll both do very well out of it.'

He rowed on for a while. Then he said, 'We've got so much in common, you and me! Let's make the most of it.'

'What have we got in common?' said Ragi warily.

'Oh lots,' said the pedlar cheerfully. 'For a start, we're both deformed: you with your flipper-feet and me with my battle wounds. Look.'

He pushed back his cloak and rolled up his sleeves. Ragi saw that his right arm was covered in raw burn-blisters. And when the pedlar wriggled the fingers on his left hand, Ragi saw that the little one was missing. In its place was a revolting, blackened stump, crusted with dried yellow pus.

'Yuck!' cried Ragi, before he could stop himself.

'My face is even worse,' the pedlar confided. 'That's why I always keep it covered up. Now, here's another thing we share in common: we would both be very happy to get hold of some treasure.'

'That's true,' said Ragi gloomily. 'I could certainly do with some treasure.'

'And that's what *my* secret is about,' said the pedlar. 'You see, I'm only *pretending* that I've come to Orkney to sell my goods. The *real* reason I'm here is this.'

He rested the oars and leaned back to rummage through his bags. At last he pulled out a flat slab of stone, not much larger than Ragi's hand. It was covered in tiny, spikily scratched rune-letters.

'What does it say?' asked Ragi.

'It speaks of a marvellous treasure,' said the pedlar excitedly. 'Listen.'

He read the inscription out, pointing at each word with his finger-stump:

ᛋᚢᚦ : ᚠᚠ : ᛒᛗᚴ : ᛒᛏᚴᚴ
'SOUTH OF BLACK BANKS

ᛁᛏ : ᛁᛋ : ᛏᛒᛗ
IT IS TOLD

ᚠ : ᛁᛏᚴᛁᛏ : ᛁᛗᚴᛏ
A JAGGED ISLAND

ᛒᛏᛉ : ᛏᛏᛏ : ᚴᛒᛗ
BARE AND COLD

26

ᚺᛒᛗᛋ : ᛏ : ᛏᚱᛒᛋ : ᛁᛚᛁᛏ

HOLDS A TROLL-MOUND

ᚠᛚᛏ : ᛒᚠ : ᛁᛒᛗ

FULL OF GOLD.

There are troll-mounds dotted all over the Orkney islands, aren't there?'

Ragi nodded.

'Well, I'm here to find the one this rune-stone speaks of, Ragi. And if you help me – I'll give you a half share of the treasure that's inside it!'

Ragi shuffled uncomfortably on his makeshift seat and gazed out at the dark sea.

'It sounds tempting,' he said. 'But how do you know it's genuine?'

'Of course it's genuine!' snapped the pedlar indignantly. 'I got the rune-stone from a very clever man.'

'Even so, it doesn't really tell you where the treasure is,' said Ragi doubtfully. 'I've never heard of a place called Black Banks.   And you're not seriously going to break into a troll-mound to get it, are you?'

'Of course I am,' said the pedlar.

'But troll-mounds are really dangerous – they're haunted!' cried Ragi. 'The trolls that live inside them are man-eaters! Their slaves are dead spirits! As you're new to Orkney, maybe you don't know this: everyone who's ever broken into a troll-mound has either gone raving mad...or the trolls and spooks have tortured them to death!'

'Well, I'm mad already,' said the pedlar cheerfully, 'so I've got nothing to fear on that score. And listen, Ragi: The man who gave me this rune-stone swore that the treasure it speaks of is nine times more splendid than anything else ever found anywhere in the North Lands! Imagine how rich we'll be, once we've got our hands on it! So. Now you've agreed to help me...'

'I haven't,' protested Ragi.

'But you've *got* to,' said the pedlar. 'Because I've already helped you by pulling you out of the sea. As Odin All-Father said: *A gift always looks for a return.* You can't argue with the chief god! Let's drink to it, eh?'

He reached under the rowing-bench and pulled out a battered leather flask and a splintery wooden cup. He poured out some beer, took a long swig through his mufflers and passed the cup to Ragi.

Ragi nearly gagged as he took it. For the pedlar's battle-scarred lips had left a revolting, black stain on the rim. Ragi pretended to drink, then quickly handed the cup back.

'Now,' said the pedlar. 'Let's work out how to get hold of this wonderful treasure. Any ideas, my friend?'

5

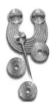

The wind was already drying Ragi's clothes. He mulled over what the pedlar had said.

He's really weird! he thought. *Best not to get involved.*

However, the pedlar had planted a hard seed of desire in Ragi's mind. Already it was sinking deep roots, and sprouting into daydreams of darkness lit by gleaming gold.

'I would like some treasure,' he said uncertainly. 'But...well, it's not just the spooks and monsters that are a problem. It's supposed to be really difficult to break into a troll-mound. The only way is by squeezing through narrow holes and long, cramped tunnels.'

'Sounds as if a big fellow like me couldn't make it then,' said the pedlar. He patted his broad chest under its thick wrapping of cloak and furs.

'I'm sure I'm too big too,' said Ragi quickly.

'You're right,' said the pedlar. 'We'll need someone very small and nimble to help us. Another child – one much smaller than you.'

He rowed on in steady silence for a while, nodding his head in time with the oars. At last he said, 'Fancy a job, Ragi – travelling round the islands as my assistant? A *double*-job. Firstly, you help me sell my goods. Secondly, when we spot a suitable child for our treasure hunt, you befriend him and bring him to me. Don't mention the mounds – just talk about the treasure. Any child would be eager to help us with *that*.'

'But that's tricking them!' said Ragi. 'Surely we ought to explain our plan properly, otherwise it's wrong...'

'Oh no!' exclaimed the pedlar. 'You're one of those irritating people who sees problems in everything. What a nuisance! Don't keep questioning and criticising me like a nagging fishwife, Ragi. I want to be friends – not throw you back into the sea.'

He slammed down the oars and stood up, panting noisily. His outstretched hands clawed at the air. His finger-stump twitched repulsively. On his feet, he seemed gigantic.

Lucky the horse is between us, thought Ragi. *Otherwise he might toss me overboard!*

He held up his fists. 'Get away!' he cried.

The pedlar's rage dissolved into a snigger. He sat down heavily. 'We could get on fine together, Ragi,' he said, 'so long as you don't make a silly, girlish fuss.'

'I am not making a...!' Ragi protested.

'Splendid,' the pedlar interrupted him. 'Because red-blooded fellows like us can't get worked up about a small bit of trickery, can we? Just think, Ragi. Together, we can win great riches and power! How can you refuse me?'

Farting giantesses! thought Ragi. *This is really tempting! But what's the heroic thing to do? Win treasure, ya, of course. Play tricks on other children – definitely not! … But on the other hand, the lads at home would stop pushing me around if I had some treasure. We could live comfortably again, just like when Pa was alive. Mam would be so proud and thrilled.*

But that reminded him of something else.

'I'm sorry, pedlar, I can't travel round the islands with you,' he said. 'You see, my mam needs me. I have to do all the heavy work around our cottage, like digging peat and fetching water.'

'Pah!' cried the pedlar. 'Crawl back to your mother then, you namby-pamby slug-a-bed!

Ragi flushed bright red. Everyone seemed to be mocking him today.

Whatever should I do? he thought. *What the pedlar's suggesting definitely isn't right. But I'll never get another chance to get so rich!*

That decided him. A big lump of guilt was still nudging at him, but he pushed it aside.

'All right,' he said. 'I'll help you.'

'Excellent!' said the pedlar. 'You can start work as soon as we reach Tide Point. And to make sure you're up to the job, have these, my friend.'

He rummaged through his bags again, fished out a pair of brand new shoes and tossed them to Ragi.

'Aw, thank you!' cried Ragi. He pulled them gratefully over his bare feet. 'What do I have to do?'

'At first it'll just involve laying out my goods, and so on,' said the pedlar. 'But once I spot a suitable child, you can help me with the treasure hunting too. Work hard, do everything I tell you, and I'll pay you well in return.'

6

The pedlar rowed up a short fjord to a straggle of small, stone cottages that formed the village of Tide Point. He hauled the boat up onto a sandy beach. Then he strapped his bags onto the horse and led it ashore, crossing a beaten mud road to a patch of open grass on the edge of the village. Ragi followed nervously.

The air had cleared and the sun was shining right overhead.

The pedlar spread a red cloth over the grass. On this he laid out a large display of tempting goods.

There were sparkling amber and glass necklaces and polished walrus-ivory combs. There were wooden images of Thor, Freyr and other popular gods, iron knives with ornate bone handles and brightly embroidered silk ribbons. There were gaming boards, bronze brooches and rings, silver Thor's-hammer pendants, fur hats and gloves, toys and trinkets.

When Ragi had helped him arrange it all neatly, the pedlar fished out a big ram's horn and blew it loudly. People hurried up from all over the village, to see what was going on.

Soon a noisy crowd of housewives, fishermen, old gaffers and children had gathered around. They pushed and shoved and fingered the goods. They haggled indignantly with the pedlar, trying to force his prices down. Ragi worked hard, keeping the display tidy and stowing silver nuggets and pennies safely in the pedlar's purse.

Eventually the crowd thinned out as the last customers carried off their purchases. The pedlar gave Ragi a hard nudge with his elbow.

'See them?' he hissed excitedly. 'They're perfect.'

'Huh?' said Ragi.

The pedlar pointed at two small figures walking across the grass towards the far bank of the fjord. 'Go after them.'

'What for?' said Ragi.

'Keep your voice down, you numbskull!' the pedlar hissed. He stepped closer, engulfing Ragi in a stomach-churning stink of rotten meat. 'They're exactly the right size for the treasure-mounds.'

Ragi screwed up his eyes to see properly. 'But they're *girls*!' he said incredulously. 'We can't use them.'

'Why ever not?' said the pedlar. 'Girls love treasure. Girls are even more stupid than me. And two will be even more useful than one. Now, listen. They were looking at the jewellery, but they couldn't afford to buy anything. Run after them, Ragi, flatter them a bit, then tell them to come back here. Say that as they clearly enjoy pretty things, I'll give them each a trinket that I've got going spare. Hurry up, before we lose sight of them.'

'But surely it's wrong to get girls involved in something so dangerous?' Ragi said uncertainly.

'Odin's eye socket!' snapped the pedlar. 'There you go again, mother's little sissy! Wrong, right, what does it matter so long as we get hold of the treasure?'

Ragi tried to interrupt him, but the pedlar ranted on: 'Pah! I wish I'd never rescued you now. Go back to the sea – Flipper-Feet!'

Ragi turned bright red. 'That's not fair!' he cried. 'When I told you my secret, you promised you wouldn't say…'

'No I didn't,' said the pedlar. 'And I'm still waiting for you to thank me for saving you from drowning. Instead you just complain and criticise me. Well, I'm not putting up with it!'

He reached under his cloak. Ragi heard the sound of metal sliding against wood... And then the pedlar drew out a very large sword!

Its blade was covered in bloodstains. The pedlar swatted it through the air – then suddenly pointed it straight at Ragi's chest!

Ragi's heart began to beat really fast. He'd never met anyone so temperamental. He'd never had a sword pointed at him before. He didn't dare move.

'Haven't I saved you from a beating?' hissed the pedlar. 'Haven't I said you can have a share of the treasure? I'm not asking much in return.'

'Sorry, sorry!' cried Ragi hastily.

And like magic, the pedlar's mood shifted back. 'Oh, all right,' he said mildly. 'Don't let's fall out. I'll forgive you. Ha ha!'

He put his sword away.

Ragi gulped. *How ever can I wriggle out of this?* he thought.

'The thing is, I'm rubbish at talking to girls,' he

mumbled. 'Supposing they don't want to come back here? I can't drag them, can I? I mean, forcing *girls* to do things...I'm not trying to be awkward, but I'm sure that's against the law.'

'*Against the law,*' The pedlar mocked him in a sing-song, falsetto voice. He snorted loudly behind his fur mufflers. 'I don't care about your Jarl's pathetic laws. Anyway, you don't need force, you need *charm*. All you have to do is recite a poem.'

'A poem?' guffawed Ragi.

'No girl – no grown woman even – can resist a poem that's full of clever words and rich promises,' the pedlar said confidingly. 'I'm a very cultured and knowledgeable man, you know. Before I lost my good looks in battle, I won over hordes of beautiful women with my poetry. Here, try this on them.'

He began to recite in a low, hoarse, voice:

> 'My friend has wondrous treasure booty,
> Kept for ones who share its beauty.
> Come! My friend will give to you
> Sea-flash gold and silver too.'

Ragi cringed. *I can't go around spouting that sort of twaddle!* he thought. Also, his conscience was badly troubling him.

But he was too wary of the pedlar's short temper to argue any more. So he jumped up and ran across the road towards the two girls, who were now sitting on the grass, looking out across the water and chattering.

7

As Ragi got closer to the girls, he felt more and more uncomfortable. *I shouldn't be doing this*, he thought. *It's bad enough tricking another lad to go into the treasure-mounds – but girls...!* He shook his head. *Girls are such weaklings – and scaredy-cats!*

He was really tempted just to clear off and never mind the chance of treasure.

But only cowards run away every time things get tricky, he thought. He was still ashamed that he'd fled the other boys on the beach.

He glanced back to where the pedlar was standing by his horse. He seemed to be watching Ragi intently.

Anyway, if I run off, he's bound to come after me with that sword! Farting giantesses! There's no way out.

So he drew himself up tall and strode resolutely

across the road and over the grass towards the girls. They stopped talking and stared at him.

They both looked younger than Ragi.

One was skinny and short with a pale face and long, wispy, fair hair, which made her look very delicate. She wore a loose, light blue dress with no belt. Her pastel-pink apron was trimmed with pretty ribbons, but they were rather grubby and half-unstitched. Her shoes were pinchy-pointy tight and the patterns on her bronze shoulder-brooches were roughly cut. Two thin chains hung from one of them, with a little bone needle-box and a bronze ear-spoon dangling from the ends. Her chest sparkled with several rows of gaudy, misshapen beads.

The other girl was taller and sturdier with very rosy cheeks. Her rolled-up sleeves showed off strong arms, like a grown-up fishwife. Her curly, brown hair was tied up in a messy topknot. She wore a cream dress and apron, plain brooches and a woven belt with a scuffed leather purse on it.

'What do you want?' the tall girl asked curtly. She folded her arms and stared at Ragi.

'I've got a message for you from the pedlar,' Ragi mumbled.

'The pedlar?' she scoffed. 'Why would we want to hear a stupid message from that ruffian?'

Ragi flinched. It was true: girls always unnerved him. He turned bright red.

'This is it,' he said. Then he launched straight into the pedlar's poem:

> 'My friend has wondrous treasure booty,
>
> Kept for ones who share its beauty.
>
> Come! My friend will give to you
>
> Sea-flash gold and silver too.'

'Oooh he wants to give us treasure, Unn!' cried the skinny girl. She clapped her hands.

'I bet he doesn't,' sneered Unn. 'You shouldn't believe a scruffy beggar like him, Cousin Kadlin.' She turned to Ragi. 'You can't fool me. Get lost!'

Ragi stared back at her. If another boy had spoken to him like that, he would have thumped him, but girls had to be treated carefully.

'It isn't nonsense,' he said. 'It's a very clever poem. The pedlar, um...he made it up, because he wants to give you some lovely jewellery – for free.'

'For *free*?' said Kadlin, twirling her dress around. 'Why?'

'It's probably some horrible tat that no one wants to

buy,' said Unn firmly. 'Just ignore him, Kadlin.' She stepped back, screwing up her face in disgust. 'Scram, you dirty pedlar's urchin!'

Ragi gave a big sigh and prepared to go. But just then Unn cried, 'Look out, boy, here come our grandparents. I'm going to tell on you. Grandpa! Grandmam!'

A boat rowed up to the beach. A white-bearded old fisherman climbed from it, then helped out a tall, grey-haired woman, who leaned on a stick. Unn ran up to them, squealing and flapping her hands about.

'Now, now, what's the matter, girls?' said Grandmam.

'This nasty boy's pestering us,' said Unn, pointing to Ragi. 'He's saying a creepy poem, telling us we're beautiful and promising us things that can't possibly be true. He's almost had Kadlin fooled.'

She put her arm protectively around her little cousin.

The old lady shook her stick at Ragi. 'A poem?' she cried. 'That's disgusting!'

'I don't think he really meant any harm,' said Kadlin in a small voice.

'Huh!' snorted Unn. 'You know Kadlin's naive,

Grandmam. Of course he meant harm. It was a dirty *love* poem.'

'It was not!' cried Ragi in horror.

'Liar, liar!' said Unn. 'Why else would you come crawling round us and chanting such nonsense unless you were trying to bewitch us with it, eh?'

Ragi stared at the two cousins in amazement. *Farting giantesses!* he thought. *They certainly are stupid if they think I'd have a crush on a clod and a weakling like them!*

But Grandmam wagged a bent finger in his face and said accusingly: 'Oh, I know your kind. Waylaying innocent young girls, treating them like floozies, *spellbinding* them with your devious words, leading them into trouble! Be off with you!'

'Ya, get away from here!' cried Grandpa.

Ragi didn't try to argue any more. He turned and sprinted away, as fast as he could.

But instead of returning to the pedlar, he ran diagonally across the grass to where another road led away from Tide Point. He jogged along it for a while, then stopped to glance back.

He saw the old couple herding the two girls back to the village. He saw the pedlar standing by his horse, still watching him.

The pedlar raised his hand in an exaggerated wave. Ragi ignored him and hurried on.

Thor's thunderbolts! he thought, *I've had my bellyful of him! I don't want his stupid treasure anyway.*

It wasn't really true. He was still burning with desire for it. But he felt sure he'd made the right decision.

Although he'd come to Tide Point by boat, he knew exactly how to get home on foot, for he'd made the journey in both directions several times before. It was a long way, but mostly flat. He could easily do it by nightfall.

He worried briefly that the mad pedlar might gallop after him, and looked back again nervously. But the pedlar seemed to have given up on him and was now leading his horse back to the boat.

Ragi felt light-headed with relief.

However, he wouldn't have been so cheerful if he'd heard what Unn and Kadlin's grandparents were saying!

'I recognise that good-for-nothing boy,' said Grandmam. 'He's Ragi Haraldsson. You know, Widow

Alfdis' son. Remember how they were both thrown off the family farm not far from here, after his father died?'

'Aha,' said Grandpa, 'that wretch!'

'Aw, Grandmam, tell us why!' begged Unn.

'No one knows the exact ins and outs of it,' said Grandmam. 'But they say an evil finman persuaded the mother to slowly poison her husband to death with her terrible cooking. You can tell the boy's under the evil influence too, pestering you with his disgusting poems, trying to spellbind you!'

'I tell you what,' said Grandpa thoughtfully, 'I have to go up to Fortress Island tomorrow to do some business in the Jarl's hall. While I'm there, I'll make a personal complaint about him to Jarl Thorfinn Skull-Splitter himself!'

8

Ragi and his mother, Widow Alfdis, lived close to the seashore in a low, oblong stone cottage with a heather-thatched roof. Like all Viking houses, it had no windows. The only opening was a plain wooden door halfway along the front wall.

Inside there was just one small room. This was simply furnished with two broad wall-benches, a wooden storage-chest and Alfdis's weaving loom.

The cottage was gloomy because they couldn't afford many oil lamps. But there was always a good peat fire smouldering away in the middle of the floor, which kept the place warm and very homely.

Alfdis gave Ragi a good telling off for disappearing all day. Then life went back to normal.

But not for long.

A few days later, Alfdis was singing loudly as she squatted by the fire, stirring a cauldron of shellfish-and-seaweed stew. She had a lovely voice and her singing was a joy to hear. But, like most of her cooking, the stew had a revolting smell.

She opened the door to let it out. And just at that moment, two horses stopped by the front yard.

A burly man, with a completely bald head and a bushy, ginger beard, jumped down from the first one. He wore a black, leather jerkin and a red cloak, with a heavy sword swinging in his shoulder-belt.

'Are you Widow Alfdis?' he barked.

'That's me,' said Ragi's mother. 'What do you want?'

Bald-and-Bushy didn't answer, for he'd already spotted Ragi coming round the corner of the cottage. Bald-and-Bushy snapped his fingers curtly at the boy.

'You must be the widow's son,' he said. 'Ragi Haraldsson, is it?'

Ragi glanced at his mother in bewilderment. She shrugged. He nodded slowly.

Bald-and-Bushy turned to help an elderly woman from the other horse. Ragi recognised her as the grandmother of the two girls at Tide Point. His heart sank into his boots.

Bald-and-Bushy pointed at Ragi. 'Is this the boy who was harassing your granddaughters?' he asked Grandmam.

She walked briskly over, leaning on her stick, and nodded severely. 'That's him for sure,' she said. 'Just look at his eyes! You can see he's sly and shifty.'

'How dare you say that about my son!' cried Alfdis.

'I'll say what I want, because I know it's the truth,' Grandmam retorted. 'It's common knowledge all over Tide Point that your kinsfolk threw you both off their farm because of your disgraceful behaviour.'

Alfdis gasped furiously.

'Shut up, women!' Bald-and-Bushy barked at them. 'Now you just listen carefully, Ragi Haraldsson.'

Ragi stared at the ground. His heart was pounding.

'I've come here from Jarl Thorfinn Skull-Splitter's hall,' said Bald-and-Bushy. 'This lady and her husband have complained about you to the Jarl. They say you've been reciting malicious love poetry to their granddaughters, trying to spellbind them and lead them astray. Is that true?'

'My Ragi would never do that!' cried Alfdis. Her face was white with shock.

'Of course I didn't,' protested Ragi. 'I was just…' He

thought quickly. '...delivering a message for a pedlar...'

'Ya and that pedlar was a rogue too,' Grandmam interrupted. 'The gloves he sold me were full of moth holes!'

'Never mind the pedlar,' Bald-and-Bushy snapped. 'It's the boy I'm dealing with now.' He turned to Ragi. 'Did you or did you not try to harm two innocent girls?'

Thoughts raced through Ragi's mind: *I didn't actually do anything wrong... It wasn't even a love poem... I was only carrying a message.*

'No sir,' he mumbled.

Bald-and-Bushy grunted irritably. 'Since he denies it, he'll have to take the Ordeal Test,' he said.

Ragi saw his mother sway slightly and clutch the cottage wall.

'Please!' she begged. 'No! My Ragi's a good boy. This is just a spiteful rumour! He'd never do anything like that. It's wrong to accuse him of things when he hasn't got a father to defend him. Give him another chance! *Please*, not the Ordeal...'

'Sorry, Widow,' said Bald-and-Bushy. 'Jarl's orders. You know he's vowed to rule these islands with an iron hand. If someone denies an accusation, he has to take the Test.'

'What...what's the Ordeal Test?' Ragi asked. But no one answered.

'I'll have to take him straight away,' Bald-and-Bushy said to Ragi's mother.

He twisted Ragi's arm up painfully behind his back and hauled him across to his horse.

Grandmam spat at Alfdis's feet. 'You rotten pair of good-for-nothings!' she said venomously. She hobbled back to her own horse with a swish of skirts. Bald-and-Bushy helped her mount it and she rode briskly away.

Alfdis began to cry.

'Ragi, how ever did you get mixed up in this?' she wailed. 'Your pa would turn in his grave if he knew...'

'I never did anything wrong!' he protested.

'Shut your face!' barked Bald-and-Bushy.

Alfdis' single cow was grazing on the scrubby grass outside the cottage. It mooed at them mournfully. Bald-and-Bushy swung Ragi roughly up onto his horse, then climbed on in front of him.

Ragi turned back one last time to see his mother weeping loudly into her apron. Then they started out along the road.

9

It was a long way to the Jarl's hall, which stood on a small island off the north-west tip of Mainland. They rode on and on, past endless fields of cattle and pigs, and several shimmering lakes. The long midsummer day faded into watery darkness. Ragi nodded off to sleep…

…And jerked awake ages later, as the horse turned sharply to the left. Ahead, the moon gleamed on the open sea.

They followed a narrow track above the shore to a low cliff. Waves broke noisily on the rocks below it. A short way across the water, Ragi saw a moving cluster of lights.

They got down from the horse. Bald-and-Bushy unpacked a picnic from his saddlebag and stuffed himself with flat bread, dried meat and beer from a leather flask. He threw Ragi the leftovers and, as soon as the boy had eaten, bound his wrists and ankles so he couldn't sneak away. Finally, Bald-and-Bushy wrapped himself in a thick cloak, lay down on the grass and went to sleep.

Ragi sat up, gazing miserably across the sea towards the twinkling lights, waiting for the night to pass. At last the dawn came up – and he could see why they had camped here.

The tide had gone out, leaving behind an expanse of rough, damp rocks. Some of these had been piled up in a snaking line to form a rough causeway. This led to a grassy, gently sloping island, where a stone village stood just above the beach.

Fortress Island! thought Ragi. *Those lights I saw in the dark must have been the watchmen's burning torches.*

At high tide it was a proper island, that could only be reached by boat. But now the tide was out, it was possible to walk across the rocks to it.

Bald-and-Bushy woke up and swigged some beer. Then he untied Ragi and forced the boy to march in front of him. Leading the horse, they went down the cliff path to the beach. They crossed over the uneven, seaweed-covered rocks, slipping and wobbling precariously.

On the far side, a short path led to the village. All the houses were big and well built, with roofs made of turf dotted with bright clumps of flowers.

Bald-and-Bushy tethered the horse to a post and led Ragi to the grandest building of all. He rapped loudly on the elaborately carved oak door. It was opened at once by a serving man, who ushered them in to Jarl Thorfinn Skull-Splitter's hall.

Ragi had never seen anywhere like it! Hundreds of oil lamps burned brightly in iron holders that hung on chains from the ceiling. The roaring peat fire was six times as big as the one in his own cottage. The walls were lined with beautifully carved wooden panelling and hung with embroidered pictures and impossibly huge weapons. The wall-benches were spread with thick, white bear furs.

Many smartly dressed men, women and children were sitting on them, talking in low tones. They were eating breakfast bowls of barley-porridge and cream. These were served by a fat woman who ladled the porridge from an enormous cauldron, steaming over the fire.

Everyone turned to see what was going on.

Bald-and-Bushy dragged Ragi to the high-seat. Framed by its magnificent pillars, there sat a tall, lean man with a neatly clipped, goatee beard and penetrating, pale blue eyes.

That must be Jarl Thorfinn Skull-Splitter, Ragi thought nervously.

Bald-and-Bushy cleared his throat. 'Here's the young wretch you had a complaint about yesterday, sir,' he said loudly. 'Ragi Haraldsson from Ebb Bay. Caught red-handed trying to spellbind two young girls with love poetry, but refuses to admit his guilt.'

The Jarl raised one eyebrow and fixed Ragi with an unnerving gaze. 'How old are you, boy?' he said loudly.

Ragi was very tempted to lie. But the Jarl's piercing eyes seemed to see right inside his head.

'Twelve, sir,' he admitted hoarsely.

'So!' said the Jarl. 'By the law of these islands, as laid down by my father, you are old enough to be responsible for your crimes. Do you admit to this accusation?'

'No!' cried Ragi. He could feel everyone's eyes on him. He wanted to die with embarrassment. But he managed to say, 'I never meant any harm to those girls. Honestly, sir! I was just running an errand for a pedlar. *He* made up that poem, not me. *He* made me say it! He tricked me! I never realised...I didn't mean to...!'

'Do you admit to this crime?' the Jarl interrupted him.

'No, sir,' said Ragi.

'Then I will have to test you by the Ordeal,' said the Jarl.

A gasp ran around the hall. The Jarl's stern face was expressionless. 'Do you know what that means?'

Ragi shook his head.

10

'It's a test of honesty,' said the Jarl. He stroked his beard with a well-manicured finger. 'Only someone telling the truth can pass it. If you fail the test, that proves you are guilty – and I will punish you. Do you understand?'

Ragi swallowed. 'Ya, sir,' he whispered.

Everyone had stopped eating. The hall was deathly silent.

The Jarl stood up and beckoned Ragi to follow him to the edge of the fire-pit.

Every eye was upon them.

Ragi's knees were trembling. He took a deep breath to steady himself.

A thick, iron bar, about the length of Ragi's forearm, lay on the ornate stones at the edge of the fire-pit. The

Jarl picked it up and tossed it into the flames. There was a soft hiss as the metal heated up.

The Jarl pressed Ragi's shoulders, pushing the boy down onto his knees.

'Reach into the fire,' he ordered. 'Pull out the bar.'

Ragi was trembling all over. Despite the heat, he felt icy cold. His hands were clammy and weak: he could hardly move his fingers.

I can't! he thought. He tried to imagine what the Jarl would do if he failed. *I suppose I'll get a terrible beating.* He swallowed heavily.

'Pull out the bar,' the Jarl commanded again.

Somehow Ragi made himself force his hands into the terrible, blinding mass of flames. The pain was excruciating. But he managed to close his fingers over the white-hot metal and pull the bar right out…

The heat cut into his flesh like a knife. He couldn't help it: he let out a shriek of agony.

'Don't let go of it yet, you cowardly wretch!' the Jarl boomed. 'Now: walk nine paces without dropping it.'

Ragi straightened up. He closed his eyes, trying to shut out the searing, throbbing pain. He took the first step.

The Jarl began to count: 'One. Two…'

Ragi felt as if his hands were on fire. With every breath he took, he could see his skin blistering and turning raw.

'...five...six...'

Almost there! he thought.

'Keep going, lad!' someone shouted.

'...seven...'

But suddenly he couldn't stand it any more. He yelped – and lost his grip.

The bar crashed heavily to the floor.

Ragi froze.

Around the hall, several voices groaned and others cheered. A woman called out, 'Hard luck!'

The Jarl barked: 'You have failed the test, Ragi Haraldsson. You good-for-nothing rascal! You have proved yourself to be guilty.'

11

'But it's not true!' cried Ragi. 'I swear by Thor – by Odin All-Father! – I didn't mean any harm to those girls. I was just…'

'Silence!' snapped the Jarl.

He strode back to the high-seat. Bald-and-Bushy dragged Ragi to stand before him.

Ragi's hands hurt so much, he wanted to cry. But he didn't.

Everyone watched and waited.

'Spellbinding young girls is a very serious crime,' said the Jarl. 'Here is your punishment, by the law of the islands, laid down by my father. You must pay fifty ounces of silver as compensation to the family of these girls.'

Ragi forced the words out: 'I'm very sorry, sir, but I

can't. We're really poor. My father's dead. My mother doesn't have any silver at all.'

'Then your kinsfolk must pay it,' said the Jarl.

Ragi stared at the floor.

Bald-and-Bushy said, 'The lad and his mother are both disowned by all their kin. There's no one to help him.'

The Jarl sat considering Ragi through narrowed eyes. He leaned over and muttered with a man on his left, rubbing his hands together impatiently.

At last he said: 'So. You refuse to pay this fine, eh?'

Ragi bit his lip. 'I...I'm not...not refusing, sir,' he stuttered. 'It's just impossible. And I didn't do...'

At a signal from the Jarl, Bald-and-Bushy clapped his hand over Ragi's mouth to silence him.

'If everyone refused my commands,' said Jarl Thorfinn, 'these islands would be completely wild and lawless. I shall use you as an example to anyone else who dares to defy me, and set you a very harsh punishment. For your menace to these innocent girls, and for refusing to pay the compensation – I declare you an *outlaw*! Do you understand what that means?'

Several of the girls and women watching gasped.

Ragi's mouth was so dry, he couldn't answer.

'Outlaw! Outcast!' said the Jarl. 'I banish you. From now on, you have even less rights than a slave.

'You have no home. I forbid everyone in these islands to help you. No one may give you food or shelter, not even your own mother. You will have to scavenge like a rat. And you'd better get hiding fast, boy – because I shall send out word that if anyone finds you, they have my permission – my *orders* – to kill you!'

12

At the Jarl's signal, the fat woman brought over a pot of ointment and a bundle of white linen strips. She spread the ointment over Ragi's burns, then bandaged his hands tightly with the linen.

He was in agony.

Bald-and-Bushy wrenched Ragi's arms up behind his back and hustled him outside. They marched up a long, grassy slope to a cliff. Far below it, the sea was dark grey and choppy, frothing with angry foam.

Bald-and-Bushy made Ragi clamber down a gully to a broad, smooth rock where several boats were hauled up. He pushed the smallest boat into the water, keeping hold of its mooring rope.

'Get in,' he said curtly.

What could Ragi do? He waded out dejectedly and

climbed into the boat. He was in a daze of shock and pain. The bandages made him clumsy and he winced in agony every time he put pressure on his hands.

A servant came down after them and handed Bald-and-Bushy a small basket. Bald-and-Bushy tossed its contents into Ragi's boat.

'Aren't you lucky?' he said sarcastically. 'Here's some stale biscuits and a flask of stagnant ditch water. See, the Jarl's not a heartless man: he's giving you a chance.' He fetched some splintery oars from another boat and waded out to pass them to Ragi. 'Now, off you go.'

He threw the rope in and gave the boat a hard shove.

'Hey, no! Hold on!' cried Ragi desperately. 'Where am I meant to go?'

The boat was already drifting out to sea.

'Nowhere!' Bald-and-Bushy called after him. He chuckled nastily. 'And if you keep going that way, you'll end up in Giant Land!'

Ragi was normally really good with boats. But his bandaged hands couldn't get a grip on the oars.

'Help!' he cried. 'In Thor's name, help me! In Odin All-Father's name! I can't manage this!'

But Bald-and-Bushy and the servant had already gone back up the gully.

The morning sun was directly behind the boat, so Ragi knew he was facing west. *I'm sure there's no land at all this way,* he thought wretchedly. *Somehow I've got to turn the boat round. Otherwise I'll fall off the edge of the world – or die of starvation!*

He lifted one hand to his mouth, gripped the bandage with his teeth and shifted it down to free the ends of his singed fingers. He did the same with the other hand. Now he could hold the tiller.

In excruciating pain, he managed to swing the boat round to face south.

He was drenched in spray and cold sweat. His shoes and trousers were soaked from wading out to the boat. His hands were agony. But he managed to get a hold on the oars and begin to row.

Slowly, slowly, he rowed away from the Jarl's island. Rowing meant sitting with his back to where he was going. The cliffs and rocks of Mainland loomed to his right. On his left was only the endless sea.

He twisted round to see what lay ahead – and let out a gasp of surprise. Another boat was coming straight towards him, moving much faster than his.

Whale puke! thought Ragi. *What should I do? If they know I'm an outlaw, they're bound to kill me straight off, just for the fun of it!* His stomach turned over. *But surely the news couldn't have spread so quickly? Maybe they'll just ignore me? Or...if I'm really careful what I say, I could even ask for help. But how, without giving myself away?*

The other boat came closer. He could see now that there was only one man in it – and a horse.

Ragi's heart sank.

The man stopped rowing and let his boat drift alongside Ragi's. Sure enough, he was wrapped against the sea-wind in a thick cloak and a fur hat with a wide brim.

Aw, farting giantesses! Ragi thought. *Not him again! What's that fool doing out here?*

It was the pedlar.

13

'Ah, good, there you are!' called the pedlar. He didn't sound at all surprised to find Ragi alone out here in the middle of the sea. 'Right. Let's work out our next step in this treasure hunt.'

Ragi was choking so much, he could hardly answer. 'You!' he spluttered at last. 'You got me into really bad trouble.'

'Never!' said the pedlar jovially.

'I was hauled up before the Jarl,' said Ragi. He bit his lip to keep the anguish from his voice. 'Those girls you made me talk to – they accused me of things. And when I denied them, the Jarl forced me to take the Ordeal Test – and I failed it! Look.'

He held up his bandaged hands.

The pedlar sniggered. 'Failed? That was stupid.'

'I couldn't *help* it,' cried Ragi. 'It was impossible! And now the Jarl's made me an *outlaw*!'

'Odin's eye socket!' said the pedlar. 'You're even more unlucky than me. An outlaw, eh? That means everyone in the whole realm is forbidden to help you, doesn't it?

Ragi nodded miserably.

'But don't worry, I'll still take a risk with you,' said the pedlar. He shifted his boat even closer, so that the side was almost bumping against Ragi's boat. His stink of rotten meat wafted pungently across. 'I'll stick by you, my friend.'

I mustn't listen to his wheedling, thought Ragi. *He's not trapping me again!*

The horse snorted loudly and let drop a piece of steaming, stinking dung. The wind had quietened, and a mist was starting to roll in from the horizon. Ragi sneaked a glance at the pedlar.

Whatever he makes out, he's up to no good. How's he managed to pop up like this, in the middle of nowhere? He's so weird! — the way he keeps clinging to me, and never showing his face. After all the trouble he's caused, I'd be mad to trust him.

He cleared his throat and said firmly, 'I'm no use to

you now I'm outlawed, pedlar. So please go away and leave me alone…'

'Nonsense!' said the pedlar. 'You're even *more* use now. I'm going to make those two girls feel really guilty about getting you into trouble. To make up for it, they'll be desperate to help us.'

'I don't want their help!' cried Ragi. 'I can manage fine on my own and I know a brilliant place to hide…'

'Really?' said the pedlar sceptically. 'Where?'

Ragi shook his head. But the pedlar kept on and on at him like an irritating mosquito's buzz:

'Tell me where,

tell me where,

tell me where!'

In the end, Ragi couldn't stand it any more.

'High Island,' he said reluctantly.

'Where on High Island, where?' insisted the pedlar. 'I need exact directions, Ragi, so I can send the girls to you with the things you need.'

'Can't you understand? I DON'T WANT YOU TO!' shouted Ragi. 'I've been to High Island loads of times before. I know good places there to fish and collect gulls' eggs and pull shellfish off the rocks. I can stone birds and pick bilberries. I've got my strike-a-light: I'll gather driftwood and light a fire to cook them.'

But the pedlar began to shake with raucous laughter. 'You can't do any of that with your damaged hands,' he honked. 'And how will you keep warm and dry when the storms come in? No, no, let the girls bring you food and blankets...'

'Why don't *you* bring them?' said Ragi.

'You numbskull!' said the pedlar. 'I can't risk coming near you on dry land. I might be spotted, and then we'd both be killed. But those girls are too young to get into trouble. Jarl Thorfinn's laws are harsh, but they don't punish whippersnappers like them. And once we've lured them to your lonely hideout, ha! We'll have them in our power. We'll send them into the troll-mound to get the treasure.'

Ragi's heart was pounding. *What can I say to get rid of him?* he thought. *He doesn't care a shrimp about right or wrong. But there must be...Ya, I know!*

'I've told you before,' he said. 'We'll never find the troll-mound where the treasure's hidden. I've never heard of that place your rune-stone mentions. We'd have to search hundreds of mounds, and that would take for ever. And anyway,' Ragi bit his lip and swallowed, then forced the next words out. 'I don't even want the treasure any more. All I want right now is to survive. And I'm sure I can do that better on my own.'

For a long moment his words hung in the air. Then the pedlar suddenly spat a stream of revolting, black saliva at him and cried, 'So you're spurning my friendship, are you? What an insult!'

He spun his boat around angrily, making the horse sway and stamp, splashing spray all over Ragi.

'Go on then,' he said. 'Wallow in your pain. Starve. I hope Odin punishes you with a really slow and nasty death. Goodbye.'

His oars flashed with lightening speed. He rowed rapidly away and disappeared into a swathe of mist.

Ragi let out a deep sigh of relief.

The mist drifted silently over the water towards him. It surrounded him, engulfed him. He couldn't see anything. He couldn't hear anything.

It was uncanny. Slowly, his relief turned to panic. The mist grew thicker.

He felt as if he was suffocating. His whole body was cold and clammy.

He couldn't help it. He couldn't stop himself:

'PEDLAR!' he yelled.

His voice sounded unnaturally loud, yet muffled by the mist. He cupped his bandaged hands to his mouth and bellowed it again:

'PEDLAR!'

For a long moment only silence answered him.

Then suddenly he heard the horse whinnying. The next moment, the pedlar's voice called back to him: 'Ragi! Have you got over your tantrum now? Do you understand, unless you accept my friendship, you'll die?'

His boat came sliding out of the mist. At first it seemed to contain only the horse, looming huge and still like a gigantic wooden carving. Then the pedlar stood up and squeezed round it towards Ragi, holding out his hands.

Ragi felt numb.

'I forgive you, Ragi,' the pedlar said. 'I will help you survive.'

'Thank you,' said Ragi wretchedly. He swallowed. 'I'll tell you where I plan to hide on High Island...'

14

The pedlar rowed away and the mist lifted.

Very, very slowly, Ragi managed to row the boat southwards. He did it like this: row ten strokes. Drop the oars and count to twenty. Row twenty strokes. Drop the oars and count to ten. Row ten strokes.... And so on. His burned fingers were raw. His hands smarted all over as if they were still smouldering.

But he didn't give up. How could he? If he gave up rowing, the currents would quickly sweep him out to sea and he would drown.

He was skirting the west coast of Mainland. He couldn't possibly land anywhere there, for people would soon find out he was the outlaw boy – and kill him.

The sun scudded in and out of clouds, moving

slowly to the west. The coast of Mainland curved away and disappeared. He crossed a stretch of open sea. At last the hills of High Island loomed into sight on his right.

Ragi drifted past its towering cliffs and narrow beaches. There was no one around. There were no other boats in sight.

He steered into the shore, jumped out and tried to haul his boat onto the beach. But before his poor, broken hands could grip it, a wave caught the boat and carried it out to sea.

'Aw! Whale puke!'

He was marooned.

The beach stretched away on either side. Above it, the cliff was as high as ten men. Gulls and kittiwakes were roosting in holes all along it. The brown stone was sheer and crumbling, impossible to climb.

He walked along, kicking his sodden shoes wretchedly through shingle and grey sand. His swollen lips were crusted with salt. He was almost deafened by the noise of waves and shrieking birds. The wind raced off the sea at him, whipping up his hair and billowing through his thin tunic. He'd lost his cloak in the boat and he was freezing.

After a while he found his path blocked by a grass-covered outcrop of rock, sloping at a steep angle from the cliff.

Ragi stepped up onto a boulder and leaped from it onto the outcrop. Then he threw himself onto his belly, used his elbows as levers and awkwardly worked his way up the slope.

'Aaagh! Awff!'

He winced and groaned every time he accidentally put some weight onto his hands. Finally he somehow flipped onto an overhanging ridge – and found himself standing safely on the cliff top.

'Phew!' he cried. 'I've survived this far!'

High Island was different from all Orkney's other islands: much wilder and bleaker. In front of him and on either side was a sweeping expanse of rough grass dotted with white and yellow flowers. There were hills in the distance. Behind him, the dark sea stretched away to the unknown edge of the world.

Ragi walked on and on, deep into the hills. He plodded through springy grass, swathes of waist-high bracken and soggy stretches of peat-bog and heather. He leaped over brown streams. He skirted round swampy lakes and ponds.

He didn't meet anyone. And that was just as well.

For news of his punishment had already travelled far from the Jarl's hall. Fishermen, ferrymen and other busybodies had carried it to every island in the Jarl's realm. Already, wind-beaten men and beefy youths were joking about what fun it would be to kill the young outlaw.

15

The next day in Tide Point was fine and sunny. However, Kadlin and Unn weren't allowed to enjoy it. Their mothers were furious with them for constantly messing around instead of getting on with their spinning. The other girls and women in their family had all gone off gathering shellfish on a nearby beach. But the two cousins had to stay at home and catch up with their work.

At least Unn was allowed into Kadlin's cottage for company. They sat side by side in the sunny doorway, twirling their spindles crossly and watching the village street.

A tall figure was ambling down it, leading a big, black horse that bulged with saddlebags.

Unn nudged her cousin. 'There's that peculiar

pedlar,' she said, unravelling a tangle of wool from her spindle. 'Doesn't he look an idiot!'

The pedlar certainly did look odd. For although it was a warm day, he was wrapped up as usual in a heavy cloak, fur mufflers and wide-brimmed hat. He made his way towards them very slowly, for he kept stopping to knock on doors and show people his goods. Quite a few villagers were buying things.

'Quickly, let's get inside before he sees us,' said Unn.

They gathered up their spindles and skeins of wool. But before they could finish, the pedlar was upon them. He stuck his foot inside the door so they couldn't close it.

'Go away!' Unn yelled at him. 'We don't want to buy anything.'

A neighbour walked past and tut-tutted at them: 'Where are your manners, girls?'

They blushed.

But the pedlar just snorted. 'Don't worry,' he said. 'I only want you to help me.'

Unn put her hands bossily on her hips. 'Help *you*? You must be joking!'

The pedlar stooped down to their level. 'It's my

boy,' he said in a hoarse whisper. He looked shiftily down the street, but no one was close enough to overhear. 'My assistant. Ragi, he's called. You remember him?'

Kadlin nodded uncertainly.

'He's a ruffian,' said Unn quickly. She grimaced. 'A horrible, slimy worm.'

'No, no, he's just a simple, innocent lad,' said the pedlar. 'I warned him over and over to stay away from girls, but he couldn't resist being friendly. And *you* couldn't resist telling nasty tales on him.'

Kadlin blushed.

'I suppose you know that your grandfather reported him to the Jarl?' the pedlar went on. 'And that the Jarl has made him an outlaw? Because of you two, the poor, friendly lad is banished and living rough – all on his own – out in the wilds!'

Kadlin gasped. 'We didn't mean to…' she said.

But Unn trod on her foot and interrupted sharply. 'Serves him right! He deserves to be punished. The way he stared at my cousin here, I'm sure he was planning to steal her jewellery.'

'What nasty children you are,' said the pedlar. 'Fancy returning a lad's friendliness by condemning him to such a terrible fate!'

'It's his own fault,' said Unn. 'He should have kept away from us.'

The pedlar ignored her. 'You must make up for this,' he said softly. 'You must help him.'

'You've got a cheek!' cried Unn. 'I hear he's got a mam who's as rotten as he is. Let her help him.'

'Impossible!' said the pedlar. 'Even an outlaw's mother is forbidden to go near him.'

'Well, he's nothing to do with us,' said Unn. 'He's your assistant. *You* help him."

'I can't, for the same reason,' said the pedlar. 'If I were caught with Ragi now, I'd be killed too – and what use would that be? No, only children as young as you are beyond the cruel reaches of the Jarl's laws.' He lowered his voice. 'Besides, even if I wanted to help, there's not much I can do because of my battle wounds.'

He showed them the stub of his missing finger.

'Eughh!' they both cried.

Then he showed them the hideous red burn-blisters on his arms.

Kadlin's eyes opened wide in horrified fascination.

Unn jumped back with a squeal. 'Stop it! You can

see my cousin's very delicate. You'll make her faint. It's revolting!'

'Ah, my dear little girls,' said the pedlar. 'How could you be so heartless?' His voice was hoarse, as if he really was in despair. 'My wounds give me constant pain.' He pulled his muffler more tightly across his chin. Only the bristles of his dark beard were visible beneath it. 'My face is in an even worse state,' he confided.

Unn flinched away. Little Kadlin stared up at him, trying to see.

The pedlar went on, 'I shall never be able to fight another battle. The only way I can earn a living these days is by travelling around selling fancy goods. And now I've lost my loyal assistant, Ragi, everything is even more difficult for me.'

'Well, don't expect us to feel sorry for you,' said Unn. 'Clear off!'

'I only want you to take the boy some food and blankets,' said the pedlar reasonably. 'That's not much to ask. And it's not far for you to go. He's hiding on High Island – just across the water from here.'

'Can't you understand?' said Unn. 'Even if he was hiding in this very village, we wouldn't dream of helping him! He's as ragged as his name, he looks as if he's never washed or combed his hair in his life, and he talks gobbledegook. He deserves everything that's come to him.'

'Surely you haven't forgotten the wise words of Odin All-Father?' said the Pedlar. '*Do not mock the traveller you meet on the road. Relieve the lonely and the wretched.*'

The girls both shuddered and looked at the ground. Odin was the most awesome of all the gods. It was dangerous to make him angry.

'Can you handle a boat?' hissed the pedlar.

'I get seasick,' said Unn at once.

The pedlar gave a honk of laughter. 'But you?' he said to Kadlin. Although his face was hidden under his mufflers, his gaze seemed to be boring into her.

'Kadlin's not allowed in boats on her own,' said Unn protectively. 'You can see she's much too weak to handle one. Not that it's anything to do with you, pedlar!'

'It's everything to do with me,' the pedlar answered. 'And you know full well that Odin All-Father watches the world and sees what everyone is doing. What excuse will you make to him, for not helping an innocent boy who *you* got into trouble?'

Neither girl answered.

'Creep out tonight,' the pedlar urged them. 'Row across to High Island. Take food and blankets to Ragi.'

'Never!' said Unn.

But little Kadlin said, 'High Island's huge. How would we find him?'

'I can tell you exactly where he'll be,' said the pedlar. He repeated the directions Ragi had given him.

Kadlin said, 'Oh, that's near the bay where your brothers sometimes take us lobster fishing, cousin.'

'Sshh!' hissed Unn.

But the pedlar had heard. 'Then it will be easy for you to find him,' he said.

'Easy?' retorted Unn. 'What, rowing all the way to High Island all by ourselves? Walking through bogs and hills in the dark? We'd be gone all night. We'd get lost. Kadlin would collapse with exhaustion. We might be pounced on by robbers or spooks. My pa will give me a whipping if he finds out, and so will Kadlin's. It's totally ridiculous!'

'Well,' said the pedlar thoughtfully. He wrapped his cloak more tightly around himself and adjusted his furs. 'If you won't help Ragi out of kindness, I wonder... Perhaps something else might persuade you.'

A gang of fisher lads strolled by. The pedlar lowered his voice again.

'How would you feel if I told you that the outlaw boy and I know where a wonderful, golden treasure is secretly hidden, eh?'

'Oh, Unn – that's what the boy said in his poem!' cried Kadlin.

The pedlar smoothed down his mufflers with his deformed hand. They couldn't help seeing his pus-crusted finger-stump. They couldn't help staring at it.

'Wonderful jewellery, fit for a princess,' the pedlar said softly. His stump twitched and throbbed grotesquely. 'Imagine, Kadlin: instead of those cheap beads, you could have pure gold sparkling on your chest and arms and fingers. You too, Unn: a bit of gold would transform you.'

He snatched his hand away and turned to go.

'Help the boy to survive,' he hissed. 'Then the treasure is yours.'

16

As soon as the pedlar had gone, Kadlin went inside, sat down on the wall-bench and smoothed her pastel skirts carefully over her knees. 'Just imagine all that wonderful gold,' she said dreamily. 'Hidden away somewhere, waiting for us!'

'Mmm,' sighed Unn. She reached down clumsily to scratch a grubby ankle. 'We'd look so beautiful in it. We'd be the most richly dressed girls in Tide Point...'

'In the whole of Orkney!' giggled Kadlin. 'And think what good husbands we'd attract when we're older, with all that treasure.'

'But we can't go off with that creepy pedlar,' said Unn.

'We wouldn't have to,' said Kadlin. 'Remember, he said we should row to High Island by ourselves.'

'But I hate boats,' said Unn. 'You know I always get seasick.'

'You'll be too busy rowing for that,' said Kadlin.

'Ya, and that's not fair,' said Unn, looking at her cousin's skinny arms. 'Because you're not strong enough to help.'

'I'll certainly try to,' said Kadlin.

'No, no,' said Unn firmly. 'You'd spoil your lovely, soft hands. You know Grandmam says they're one of your best marriage prospects.'

'Huh,' said Kadlin. 'I wouldn't need soft hands if I had the treasure.'

'But that boy,' said Unn. 'He's not just big and strong, he's an *outlaw*, Kadlin – really dangerous.'

'I don't reckon he is,' said Kadlin. 'Didn't you see him squirm when he spoke to us? He's just pathetic. *Please*, let's do it, Unn. I can't stop thinking about all that gold.'

Unn sighed. 'I know, me too. But it's such a risk...'

'It doesn't take long to get to High Island,' said Kadlin. 'If we went as soon as everyone's asleep, we'd be back before morning.'

'Well,' said Unn. 'I suppose we could take him a few rubbishy things. Just enough to make him think we're trying to help....'

'My mam's got some threadbare old blankets she won't miss,' said Kadlin. 'And I'm sure we can both find some leftover food.

Unn giggled. 'Ya, stuff that's going rotten. We'll be off before he even notices, because we'll make him give us the treasure straight away.'

17

The people of Tide Point all lived in small, windowless cottages above one side of the fjord. Each family slept side-by-side and head-to-toe under blankets and sheepskins on their wall-benches.

That night, almost everyone in the village was sleeping deeply. But Kadlin and Unn both lay wide awake, day-dreaming about the pedlar's wonderful treasure hoard.

Kadlin waited on tenterhooks until her parents and younger brothers and sisters were all snoring. Then she threw off her blankets and slid from the bench. The banked-up fire glowed, dull and red. She dressed quickly, opened the door and slipped out.

It was very late, but not yet quite dark.

Kadlin fetched two torn, doggy-smelling blankets

from a hiding place in the yard. Unn crept clumsily out to join her from the cottage next door, carrying a basket of stale food.

They hurried along the path, whispering and giggling. The twilight darkened.

At the top of the short fjord, several small boats were hauled up on the beach. The girls found one with their family mark – a rough picture of a fish – scorched into the wood. They pushed it down to the water and climbed inside. They took an oar each and rowed clumsily out of the fjord to the open channel.

The night was clear. The moon and stars shone brightly. They began to cross the sea.

A fishing boat passed them on its way back to Tide Point, but the crew was too busy to notice them. After that, they didn't see any other boats at all.

It was really lonely. Their oars splashed and echoed between the islands.

Kadlin tried her very hardest to row. But she was so puny, her oar barely even skimmed the water. So Unn really did end up doing nearly all the work. She grumbled and sighed loudly; but at least the effort stopped her being seasick.

They were both bubbling with excitement about the treasure.

At last they reached High Island. They landed in a sandy bay, secured the boat, took the basket and blankets and ran up a grassy slope. Already the first streaks of dawn were lighting the sky.

The two girls followed the pedlar's directions to a narrow valley between two steep hills. They walked on, looking out for landmarks, peering up every stream they saw tumbling down the hillside.

At last, in the chilly morning twilight they spotted one fringed by something very unusual in Orkney: a clump of small trees, no taller than they were.

'That must be it!' said Kadlin excitedly.

They clambered up the bank beside the tumbling water.

And just as the pedlar had promised, curled up under the trees, there was Ragi.

18

Ragi woke up with a start. His stomach rumbled loudly. He stared at the two girls in confusion.

I don't believe it! he thought. *This time, the pedlar's actually kept his word.*

Unn held out her basket.

'Here, we've brought you some food, outlaw boy,' she said coldly.

Ragi jumped up, tore it from her hands and scrabbled inside it. He pulled out a clutch of broken barley biscuits and stuffed them into his mouth. He munched and swallowed too quickly; he choked and burped. Then he found a hunk of mouldy cheese and gobbled that down too.

'Thor's thunderbolts!' hissed Unn. 'Look at him, Kadlin. He eats like a dog. He really is a piece of rubbish – just like Grandmam said.'

'Sshh!' whispered Kadlin. 'You can't blame him: he must be starving. Anyway, don't let him hear us insulting him, or he might not give us the treasure.'

'He will,' retorted Unn. 'The pedlar said so. He's *got* to.'

Kadlin turned to Ragi and flashed him a nervous smile. 'Eat up, she said. 'There's plenty more still in the basket. And look, we've brought you some blankets to keep you warm and cosy. Here, we'll make you a bed.'

She nudged Unn. Together the girls spread out the mangy, old blankets on a bare patch of earth under the tree.

'Here's a pillow for you,' said Unn sarcastically. She placed a large stone at one end of the blankets.

Kadlin quickly plonked some moss on top, to make it soft. But Ragi was too busy devouring a smelly dried fish from the basket to care.

The two girls danced around, giggling. They edged the makeshift bed with a pile of dead heather and twigs. 'Look Ragi,' said Kadlin. 'We're building you a proper hideout to sleep in.'

All three children were totally engrossed in what they were doing. So none of them heard the horse that came cantering along the valley bottom. None of them noticed it stop. None of them saw a tall figure leap from its back and start up the steep bank towards them...

Until a shadow suddenly blocked out the rising light.

Ragi's mouth dropped open. A half-chewed lump of fish and saliva dribbled out onto the grass.

The two girls spun round – and screamed.

'Pedlar!' cried Ragi. He backed away, rubbing his belly and burping. 'What are you doing here? You said it was too dangerous to come near me again.'

The pedlar seemed gigantic, silhouetted against the bright morning light. His stink of rotten, maggoty meat wafted from the folds of his cloak. He adjusted his fur mufflers. He pulled his hat forward so that even his prickly beard was swallowed by its shadows. He rumbled with laughter.

'Aren't you pleased to see your old friend, Ragi?' he said.

Ragi shuddered.

But Unn held out her hand brazenly. 'Where's the treasure you promised us in return for coming here, pedlar? Come on, hand it over.'

The pedlar didn't move.

Kadlin whispered in Unn's ear, 'Don't be daft. Treasure hoards are always stored in huge wooden chests. He'll have to bring it from wherever it's hidden to our boat... And when we get back to Tide Point, we'll have to get one of our pas to carry the chest home for us. Ooh, I can't wait!'

'Obviously, the treasure isn't actually *here*,' said the pedlar. 'If it was, Ragi would have taken it already. He would have used some of it to pay a fine to the Jarl, to free him from being an outlaw.'

Unn put her hands on her hips. 'Well, wherever it is, you'd better go and fetch it at once, pedlar – after all the trouble we've gone to, helping your boy.'

'Right,' said the pedlar. 'I shall tell you exactly where it lies buried.'

Ragi stared at him in surprise. *So he knew all along!* he thought.

'I'll take you to the very spot in my boat,' the pedlar went on. 'Then you can fetch it out yourselves.'

'We're not going in your boat!' protested Unn. 'It was bad enough rowing here, and I know for sure I'll be seasick if I have to go any further. And if the treasure's buried, we're not digging it up. You can see

Kadlin's not strong enough.'

'Anyway,' said Kadlin, gazing boldly up into the thick shadows of the pedlar's hat. 'The whole point is, you promised to *give* it to us.'

'But instead, you're trying to cheat us out of it,' said Unn. She folded her arms across her chest indignantly. 'We've done exactly what you said, even though it meant taking all sorts of risks. So go and fetch the treasure you owe us – RIGHT NOW! Go on, pedlar!' She snapped her fingers like a noblewoman ordering a slave.

Kadlin giggled.

'I don't think you quite understand,' said the pedlar. An ugly, rough edge was creeping into his voice. 'This is *my* game. I make the rules, not you. Ragi realises that, don't you Ragi?'

Ragi shrugged.

'Oh, don't try and wriggle out of it,' the pedlar goaded him. He waved his finger-stump in Ragi's face, to make the point. 'You're itching to get hold of this treasure hoard just as much as these two girls, aren't you?'

'What?' cried Unn. 'But you promised the treasure to *us* – as our reward for helping him. If he's allowed some of it, that's not fair!'

'Don't worry, there will be plenty enough to go round,' said the pedlar. 'But Ragi's too big to fetch it himself, you see. He can't fit into the tunnel that leads into the troll-mound where it's hidden.'

'*Troll-mound*?' cried Kadlin

'Don't sound so shocked,' said the pedlar. 'Surely you must have realised that's what we were talking about? Where else in these islands would a great treasure be hidden without someone already getting their hands on it? I brought you two girls into our quest, to go down the tunnel and fetch it out for us. But if you don't want to...well, that's a shame, but it's not the end of the game.'

'This is disgraceful, pedlar,' said Unn. 'We would never have agreed to come out here if we'd realised you were going to send us into a troll-mound!'

'Liar,' said the pedlar. 'As soon as you heard about this treasure, you both wanted it so badly, nothing would have stopped you. You're like greedy pigs when it comes to gold and silver.'

'How dare you say that!' cried Unn.

'Because it's true,' said the pedlar. 'Isn't it, Kadlin Sparkle-Beads, my dainty little beauty? You've been dreaming day and night of flashing all the jewellery around.'

Kadlin flushed scarlet. But she didn't deny it.

'So, as you want it so badly, I'll give you another chance,' said the pedlar. 'Instead of fetching the treasure yourselves, you can help me and Ragi to catch some other children to go into the mound for us.'

The two girls gawped at him in astonishment.

'The spooks and monsters that live inside it will probably kill them, of course,' said the pedlar. 'But that won't matter, as long as the brats throw the treasure out to us first.' He gave a honk of laughter.

'What...what exactly are you saying now, pedlar?' cried Unn. She wasn't blustering any more: she was trembling. 'Surely you're not suggesting that the only way we can get this treasure...'

'That you've *promised* us!' little Kadlin threw in.

'...that the only way,' said Unn, 'is by throwing some other children to the trolls?'

'That's disgusting!' shrieked Kadlin.

'Oh, don't worry, trapping other children is very easy,' said the pedlar smoothly. 'Isn't it, Ragi?'

Whale puke! thought Ragi, *These two girls must think I'm a monster like him!* He felt utterly ashamed. He screwed up his eyes, wishing the ground would swallow him up. *Thunderbolts! But I dare not disagree with the pedlar now, or he might fly into another rage and attack us all with his sword.*

The pedlar went on: 'It's not a suggestion. It's an order. You're so greedy for this treasure, that I'm not letting you go home without it. You either fetch it from the troll-mound yourselves, or you bring me some other children to do it.'

Unn's lip was trembling. She looked as if she was about to burst into tears.

'We're not doing this!' cried Kadlin. 'It's disgusting! Come on, Unn, let's go home!'

'Home?' said the pedlar. 'What, to spend all day in your pokey cottages doing the spinning that you hate so much? Oh no, my little beauties, once you have joined my game, you will soon have enough treasure to buy your own farms!'

Kadlin clutched her cousin's hand, but she continued to stare defiantly up at the pedlar's hidden face.

'Stop it!' she shrieked. 'Shut up! No, we won't do what you say!'

'I don't want this silly treasure any more,' sobbed Unn. 'You're right, Kadlin, let's go.'

The two girls started to pick their way down the

slope. At once, the pedlar leaped ahead and flung out his arms to stop them.

'Get out of our way!' screeched Kadlin.

She dodged under the pedlar's arms, but he twisted round and easily grabbed her thin little shoulder. Unn tried to prise his hand off her cousin, but his huge fingers were like strips of iron and his ghastly stump made her flinch. Kadlin wriggled like a butterfly caught in a net. But the pedlar only laughed and tightened his grip.

'Since you refuse to cooperate,' he growled, I shall lock you inside the mound and let the spooks tear you to pieces!'

'Let go of my cousin, pedlar,' Unn screamed at him. 'Otherwise I'll…I'll…'

'"Tell on me"?' the pedlar mocked her in his falsetto voice. 'Who to, in this deserted place?'

'I'll bite you!' Unn screamed.

She opened her mouth and leaned towards the pedlar's hand. But as she neared him, the pedlar's foul, maggoty smell made her gag. His rotten finger-stump twitched and oozed out a thick bubble of yellow pus. She froze, then backed away.

'You're both brutes!' she sobbed, and pointed at

Ragi. 'No wonder they made you an outlaw!'

'Ya,' said the pedlar, 'we're as bad as each other, eh, Ragi? I think it's time to tell them why I keep my face hidden, don't you?'

Ragi was hopping uncomfortably from one foot to the other. 'Because of...your battle wounds?' he mumbled.

'What battle wounds?' the pedlar mocked him.

'Oh!' gasped Kadlin suddenly. 'Goddess Freyja's amber tears! I've just realised! What fools we've been!'

She tried again to shake off the pedlar's grip, grimacing desperately as he dug his fingertips deeper into her bony shoulder.

'Don't you remember, Unn? Last Yule feast – that storyteller from Norway recited a long piece – it was really scary – about an evil man with a hidden face like his...'

'*That?*' said Unn incredulously. 'But it was only a story – like the one about the dragon. Surely that villain can't be *real*?'

'But Grandpa said,' whispered Kadlin. 'He *warned* us. If only we'd listened...'

Wind gusted down the valley.

The pedlar stood stock still, legs astride.

'Why do you think I've put so much effort into luring you pathetic children into my trap?' he hissed. 'Why am I drooling at the thought of throwing you to a slow and horrible death in a troll-mound? Oh my young friends, I am licking my lips at the thought of gobbling you up once the spooks have torn you to pieces! Ya indeed, I am the stuff of storytellers' nightmares, the one that every child dreads meeting.

'I am the mighty Grim Gruesome!'

19

Ragi just stood there gawping at the pedlar – at Grim Gruesome! – in astonishment.

'*You* never really trusted me either, did you Ragi?' hissed Grim Gruesome. 'You never felt comfortable with me. You tried so hard to throw me off, but I clung to you like a leech. Ha! My little friend, my trusted assistant! My child-snatching game is so much more fun since you agreed to help me lure other young victims into my trap.'

'I never…!' cried Ragi.

'Oh, but you did,' said Grim Gruesome. 'You let me save your life when I pulled you from the sea. In return for that, by Odin's law, you must agree to everything I ask. And what I ask is this: bring me other children to enslave and torment!'

He released his grip on Kadlin... Then suddenly he flashed his pus-crusted finger-stump before the girls' faces. It throbbed, twitched and wriggled repulsively.

'Don't look at it!' whispered Kadlin.

The girls screwed their eyes shut. But Grim Gruesome had already turned to Ragi again.

'You've proved your talent for the task, my boy,' he said. 'You've lured these two girls here as easily as flies to rotten meat. My mouth is watering! Think how many other children we can catch together.'

Kadlin nudged Unn. 'Quickly!' she muttered. 'While he's got his back to us... We could get away.'

She dropped lightly onto her backside and shuffled off through the heather, heading down the slope. Unn hesitated, then followed clumsily.

Meanwhile, Ragi was saying in desperation, 'But I won't be any use to you, now I'm an outlaw.'

'Rubbish!' roared Grim Gruesome. 'I shall disguise you. Not even your own mother will recognise you.'

He pulled out his sword and held the blade teasingly to Ragi's throat. 'This is your choice, Ragi,' he hissed. 'Work with me – or die!'

'But what you're asking me to do – it's wrong!' Ragi protested.

'How can anything be "wrong" for someone who is already outlawed?' Grim Gruesome mocked him.

Ragi prayed silently, desperately to mighty Thor, the god who protected good people. *Give me strength to resist him!*

But Grim Gruesome's voice droned on, drowning out his good intentions: 'Don't throw away your young life, Ragi. Instead, enjoy the glory of sharing power with the most dreaded villain in the North Lands!'

Silently, surreptitiously, the two girls reached firm ground at the bottom of the valley. There was a proper path here. If they ran now, they might really escape!

Don't give in to him! Ragi thought wretchedly. *Mam would be so ashamed! And Pa too, if he was still alive...* Bile rose in his throat. He swallowed it manfully, but at once another dark thought jolted him. *Ya, but Mam will be even more devastated if I die...!*

Suddenly the horse began whinnying. And from a short way off, there came a terrible screaming.

20

Grim Gruesome grabbed Ragi's arm and dragged him downstream to the valley bottom. A shaft of watery sunshine leaked over the hill. A short way along the rough path, Ragi saw Kadlin and Unn sprawled on the mud, clutching their legs, sobbing and groaning.

Grim Gruesome's horse was standing over them, one hoof raised threateningly, its lips drawn back to reveal vicious-looking teeth.

'What's it done to them?' Ragi blurted.

'Not "it",' growled Grim Gruesome. 'My horse is a "he". Make sure you remember that. His name is Haski, and he's showing these pathetic creatures that there is no escape.'

He strode over to the girls. 'Get up!'

They struggled to their feet shakily.

'Don't be afraid of me, little darlings,' said Grim Gruesome using his simpering, falsetto voice again. 'Join me. Help me. Don't worry, you won't get caught. No one would ever suspect girls – especially feeble girls like you – of helping the most powerful villain in the North Lands! What a team the four of us will make together!'

'Should we…?' Unn whispered fearfully.

Kadlin shook her head firmly and clapped her hand over her cousin's mouth. 'Shut up!' she shrieked at Grim Gruesome. 'What you're suggesting is…it's unspeakable. We wouldn't dream of harming other children…!'

'Liar!' roared Grim Gruesome. 'You were happy enough to tell tales and harm Ragi – weren't you?' He laughed; his old, foolish honk dissolving into a ghastly, grating bellow that seemed to freeze the children's blood. 'So you're stupid enough to refuse this wonderful chance, eh? Then I'll throw you to the trolls.'

Ragi stared at the heather and bracken. A macabre picture flooded into his mind: the two girls in suffocating darkness, surrounded by flickering, gyrating trolls and ghosts.

I don't want to be involved in torture and killing! he thought. *But what can I do to stop Grim Gruesome? Nothing! And I'm puking well not risking my life to help those two spiteful prigs – not after they told on me and got me outlawed.*

He could feel Grim Gruesome's eyes on him – the eyes he had never yet seen, lost in the impenetrable shadows of his mufflers and hat.

Thunderbolts and dwarf spit! I've got to save myself – and quickly! thought Ragi.

So he strode boldly forward – and kicked Unn, hard.

She squealed and tried to thump him back. But Grim Gruesome waved his sword in her face, making her shrink away.

'A good start, Ragi,' Grim Gruesome hissed at him.

Ragi was cringing inside at what he'd done. But he desperately didn't want to die. So he forced himself to shout, 'Thank you, Grim Gruesome, I'm with you!'

21

Grim Gruesome unrolled a length of coarse sailcloth from his saddlebag. He grabbed the girls by the scruffs of their necks, rolled them inside it and secured the cloth in place with thick ropes. Then he fixed the bundle behind his horse, like common goods on a makeshift sledge.

Ragi could hear them sobbing and moaning. He gritted his teeth and hummed loudly to himself to shut out the horrible noise.

Grim Gruesome swung himself onto the saddle and beckoned Ragi to mount behind him. The villain dug in his heels and Haski set off down the valley at a brisk pace. The girls screamed as they were dragged along after the horse.

At the valley end they reached a proper beaten-mud

road. But the horse leaped straight across it and went on, across the wild moor.

Kadlin and Unn were jerked and bumped roughly along the ground. Soon they were a mess of scratches, sores and bruises. Through gaps in the cloth, they made out green and brown patterns whizzing past, as the horse sped over the wild land. But Ragi saw great stretches of heather and bog, waist-high bracken and desolate ponds.

At length they heard the shrieking of gulls and smelled the tang of the sea. Haski emerged onto a grassy cliff. Grim Gruesome leaped down and ordered Ragi to follow suit. Grim unbundled the girls and grabbed them in his huge arms. He jumped down to a ledge with them and picked his way across some flat rocks.

Grim Gruesome's boat – the same he had used in his guise as a pedlar – was moored there. He tossed the girls into it like sacks of flour.

Unn squatted in the bottom of the boat and buried her sobbing face in her hands. But skinny Kadlin pulled herself upright. She seized her cousin's hand and tried to climb out.

'Stop them, Ragi!' Grim Gruesome hissed.

Ragi waded out into the water. Never mind his damaged hands: his elbows and feet were strong enough to force the girls back into the boat.

Unn choked back her tears. 'You bully!' she shrieked at him.

'Ya!' Kadlin piped up. 'You disgraceful lump of pig poo! I was a fool to feel sorry for you. Whatever would your mam say if she knew what you were doing?'

Don't listen, Ragi told himself. *Think of that treasure!*

Unn's face was red and streaked with tears. 'She'd call you a COWARD!' she spat. 'Attacking helpless girls! Siding with a villain because you're too afraid to stand up to him!'

'Ya,' said Kadlin. Her skinny body was trembling from head to toe, but her voice was steady. 'After we risked everything to help you... You should be *saving* us from Grim Gruesome!'

Now they started yelling at him together: 'Coward, coward, COWARD!'

Coward. It was the most insulting word anyone could say to a Viking boy.

Everyone says that about me, Ragi thought wretchedly. *The lads at home, the Jarl, these girls...*The word slashed at his heart like a knife. *Don't listen, don't*

*listen! It's not my fault! I was only trying to save myself...
And they betrayed me, they got me outlawed... Aw, but
dwarf spit! That's no excuse. Remember Pa telling me about
how girls need protection... He'd think I was despicable –
he'd turn in his grave – if he knew I'd sent two to their
death, just to save my own life!*

He was standing knee-deep in the icy water. Grim
Gruesome waded out to him, reached into the boat and
handed Ragi a stout club. It was like the sticks the lads
on the beach had fetched to kill the seal all those days
ago.

'Beat them with this until they shut up,' Grim
Gruesome growled.

Ragi gripped the club between the bandages of his
two hands. He swung his arms up to get some
momentum...

But he couldn't do it.

He dropped the club. It fell into the sea with a
splash. And a great weight seemed to slip off his
shoulders.

He drew himself up tall. He turned to face Grim
Gruesome. If only he could see the mysterious features
that lay beyond the dark shadows of the outsized hat
and furs!

'I've changed my mind,' he said. 'I'm not helping you, Grim Gruesome, I'm NOT!' His voice had gone all squeaky like a girl's, but he didn't care. 'I'm not going to become a brute like you. I'm not going to save my own skin if it means turning into a monster!'

He wasn't afraid now. In fact, he felt stronger than he'd ever felt in his short life.

Kadlin and Unn tried to clamber out of the boat again. But Grim easily pushed them both back in, sloshing water carelessly into Ragi's face. He led Haski into the boat, leaped in himself and pushed away from the shore.

'Stay here and wallow in your misery, Flipper-Feet!' he bellowed at Ragi. 'And while you wait for the folk of High Island to find you and stone you to death for being an outlaw, think about the mess you're in. *You* lured these girls into my trap, Ragi, whatever excuses you make. Thanks to *you*, they'll die a slow and horrible death. It's no good changing your mind now. Your evil deed is already done!'

The girls were both yelling something at Ragi. But he couldn't make it out before Grim Gruesome took up the oars and rowed quickly away.

22

I've got to save them! thought Ragi in a panic. *Aw, but dwarf spit! I've no idea where he's taking them. The only way is to follow them!*

He waded further out, squelching clumsily in the shoes the pedlar had given him. They'd been waterlogged so many times, now he could feel them disintegrating and dissolving away. Without them, his webbed feet smarted on the sharp shingle. The sea-bed sloped steeply and he was soon out of his depth, but he managed to tread water. The food the girls had given him had renewed his strength.

He began to swim. Even his smarting hands didn't hold him back now. His strong arms tore through the waves. And the tide was on his side: it carried him after the boat almost effortlessly…

But he'd forgotten how treacherous the sea can be. He'd reckoned without the currents.

Suddenly he found himself caught up in a seething mass of water that tugged and dragged at him until he felt that his whole body would be torn in two. He struggled fiercely against it.

A great wave hit him full in the face and dragged him under.

Then all he knew was liquid darkness. And he realised he was about to drown.

23

'Urgh! Ooargh! Yearrgh!'

Unn was kneeling at the side of Grim Gruesome's boat, being violently sick into the sea. 'Awf! I'm puking up all my insides. I feel so dizzy and faint. I want to die!'

Kadlin squatted beside her and put a comforting arm round her cousin's shoulders. Both girls' clothes were filthy, torn and dishevelled, like beggars.

'Mind out,' gasped Unn. She heaved again. 'Awoomph!'

'I'm so sorry,' whispered Kadlin tearfully. 'It's all my fault. Oh, if only I hadn't wanted the treasure so much!'

'I wanted it just as badly as you,' groaned Unn.

Kadlin twisted a strand of her lank, tangled hair

wretchedly round her fingers. 'I honestly don't want it any more,' she said.

'Nor do I...'

A shadow fell over them. 'But *I* want the treasure, my beauties,' said Grim Gruesome.

He squatted beside them, the wind flapping his cloak against Unn's vomit-stained dress. He was monstrously huge. His rotting meat smell was overpowering. He flaunted his finger-stump in front of Kadlin's face, then pulled it away with a rasping laugh.

'Let's play the game one more time, little girls. Go on, prove yourselves bolder than namby-pamby Ragi. Bring me treasure from the mound before the trolls attack you – and perhaps I will still let you go free.'

'I don't believe you,' choked Unn.

'Ha! Then perhaps I won't, Unn Sharp-Tongue,' Grim Gruesome answered her. 'That's all part of the fun.'

He stood up and began to stomp around the boat, muttering crazily. 'No treasure, no chance. Enough treasure gives you a small chance – depending on how ravenous I am to hear your screams and gnaw the flesh from your dead bones. But for the best chance of all, you must agree to help me trap other children – as many as I want – and lure them to the troll-mound. Do that, my pretty darlings, and I will turn the boat around at once.'

His voice grew louder.

'Think of it! I'll guard you both. I'll free you from your pathetic old lives. And the more children you trick into my power, the bigger your share of the treasure.'

Haski gave a loud snort and began to wave his tail about. Grim Gruesome strode along the boat and fumbled in his bags for some oats to feed the horse.

'Kadlin,' Unn whispered urgently. She clutched the boat's side and spoke between vomiting. 'Do you think... Yearrgh! ...that we *should* agree to trap some other children? I mean, if that's the only way to save ourselves...?'

'No!' said Kadlin hoarsely. 'That would be terrible!'

'I know it's wrong,' said Unn. 'But I'm so scared. I don't want to die...'

'If we trapped other children,' said Kadlin, 'we'd be as bad as the outlaw boy. Everyone would hate us. You know what Grandmam says...'

'Ya,' sighed Unn. '"It's always better to die with a

good reputation, than to live and have people despise you."'

'Exactly,' said Kadlin. 'Anyway, don't you realise? If we agreed to join Grim Gruesome, he'd have complete control over us. We'd be his slaves!'

A furious wind blew up. Grim Gruesome had raised an ugly black sail that billowed and flapped like an ill-omened crow. The sea was a frothing, churning whirlpool. Enormous waves rocked the low-slung boat and surged onto the shallow deck. There was no sign of land in any direction.

Kadlin sat silently, shivering inside her cloak, her skinny arms wrapped around her knees, her delicate face buried in the grubby folds of her pastel-pink apron.

Unn had no more sick inside her. She sprawled uncomfortably in the bottom of the boat, groaning. Her dress, cloak and apron were all stained with vomit, and her curly hair had come undone from its topknot.

They were both soaked through.

Grim Gruesome stood in the back of the boat, grasping the tiller as if he were trying to strangle it.

But the gale was stronger even than he was. It

caught the sail with invisible, iron hands and spun the boat round and round, lurching violently.

Grim Gruesome wrestled the sail down. Then he grabbed the oars, and rowed fiercely against the swell, grunting and cursing. Kadlin huddled beside Unn, praying silently to Thor.

By the time the windstorm finally quietened, a strange, hilly land had appeared under the clouds to the left.

'Wolf guts!' Grim Gruesome swore. 'We've come through to the wrong side. Ach! We'll have to go the long way round the top end of these islands to reach the troll-mound.'

He squatted close to the girls and dropped his voice.

'Never mind, my little darlings. It'll give you longer to make yourselves ill with worry, eh? Ya, longer to tremble over the darkness of the mound, and all the other terrors I have planned for you!'

24

Day turned to night and then to day again. They sailed through soft, grey rain, up a craggy coastline, unlike anywhere the girls had ever been before. They had no idea where they were. They skirted a northerly headland and began to make their way down the other side.

At last Grim Gruesome rowed into a channel fringed by low hills. He steered the boat inland to the head of a jagged fjord.

No houses. No people. No animals.

They landed on a small beach. Grim Gruesome forced the girls out of the boat and up a slope covered in coarse grass, heather and rocks. On the way they stopped to drink from a peat-brown stream. He fed them on dirt-tasting biscuits from Haski's saddlebags, allowing them to eat as many as they could manage. Then he seized their hands and dragged them up a low hill.

The wind screamed through the loneliness. They were both too weak to try and resist him.

Just before the top, they came to a large, grass-covered bump as high as two men. There was a bare patch on one side of it, filled by an enormous rock.

Grim Gruesome shoved the girls aside, drew his sword, rammed it into the joint between the rock and the grass and levered it around. The rock loosened with a soft creak. He hauled it away with his bare hands. Underneath was a small, black hole.

Grim Gruesome grabbed Kadlin and then Unn, and pushed them both easily into the hole. Then he tossed two small, hard things in after them.

'Here's a strike-a-light and a torch-stick to help you find your way,' he called. 'Crawl right inside the mound, my little darlings. If the trolls don't pounce on you straightaway, bring me all the treasure you can find in there. When I see what you've got, I shall decide what to do with you.'

He rolled the entrance rock back into place.

25

Ragi floated on the waves like a dried twig. He was helpless. He was unconscious. But he wasn't alone.

For the sea around the Jarldom of Orkney was as busy as the land. Whales swam through it. Dolphins fished and dived. And seals moved endlessly between the shore and the water.

A group of seals saw Ragi bobbing up and down in the waves. They swam over to investigate. They circled him. Their round faces gazed at Ragi with soft, unblinking eyes. They soothed his senseless ears with mysterious sounds.

The tide began to flow in. Slowly the seals guided the unconscious boy through it, up the coast of High Island, past rocks and cliffs, to an open bay with a sandy beach.

And there they left him, safe above the water line. He was cold, wet and lost to the world.

But he was still alive.

26

Ragi woke up – and jerked back with a gasp. Standing over him was a huge and hideously revolting man. He was crooked and stooped, with a huge, lumpy hump on his back. His face was twisted into a fearsome grimace. His eyebrows were like bristly twig-brooms. Blackened teeth protruded lopsidedly from one corner of his mouth. His squashed, puffy nose seemed spread all over his face.

Ragi's stomach turned to water and his heart pounded.

Whale puke! he thought. *It's Grim Gruesome! No wonder he normally hides himself.*

Ragi forced himself to stare back defiantly. The monstrous face edged closer. Its twisted mouth opened in a grotesque grin.

Ragi was lying underneath a pile of old furs. He was on a bench right up against a solid wall. They were in a small, untidy, softly lit room, with smouldering peats glowing red in the fire-pit. The door was tightly shut. There was no escape!

Ragi bit his lip so hard, it bled.

Don't let him see I'm scared, he thought. *Put up a fight!*

He pushed off the covers and sat up queasily.

He was light-headed with thirst and hunger. The bandages had come off his hands and they felt itchy now, rather than sore. He didn't seem to have any fresh wounds.

He swung his legs down to the floor and managed to stand up.

The monstrous man burst out laughing.

And Ragi almost fainted with relief. That wasn't Grim Gruesome's crazy, rasping croak. This man had a good, warm-hearted chuckle. He saw now that, instead of the ghastly stump, the man had five full fingers on each hand. And under the bristly brows, his eyes were twinkling with good humour. It wasn't Grim Gruesome after all!

'Eh, don't worry, everyone gets a fright when they first see me,' said the man. He had a deep, sing-song voice. 'But so what? We're all different. You'll soon get used to me.' He chuckled again. 'I'm Otkel,' he went on. 'Everyone calls me Mushroom-Nose. I don't need to tell you why.'

Ragi's head was swimming. He sat down heavily again.

'Are you hungry?' asked Otkel. He sounded very friendly.

Ragi nodded and looked around hopefully for the woman of the house. But no one appeared.

'I'm afraid there's only me lives here,' said Otkel Mushroom-Nose. His ghastly face creased into another grin. 'You don't seriously think any woman would agree to marry an ugly oaf like me, do you? But I'm a dab hand at cooking. And I've just caught some fine haddock.'

He stoked up the fire and set a flat stone to heat on it. Then he scooped a big, silvery fish from a bucket. He gutted it slickly with his knife, split it open, sprinkled it with herbs and laid it on the hot stone.

The fish sizzled away. Otkel took a small set of wooden pan pipes from his belt and played a cheerful tune. Then he scooped the fish into a wooden dish and handed it to Ragi with a wink.

Ragi wolfed it down. 'That was the best meal I've ever had!' he said, wiping his mouth with his hand. 'Thanks, Otkel Mushroom-Nose. And thank you even more for rescuing me. I think...I nearly drowned, didn't I? How ever did you find me?'

Otkel was cooking another fish. 'You were washed up on the beach,' he said, 'in the middle of the night. I often go prowling round when all the other folk are asleep. They appreciate it because I keep an eye out for robbers and pirates. Even better, being nocturnal, I keep my ugly mutt out of sight. Lucky for you, eh? Thirsty?'

Ragi nodded.

Otkel handed him a wooden cup of warm, frothing milk. 'I might not have a wife, but I've got a fartingly good cow!' he said. 'Now then, lad, I'm going to talk straight with you. As soon as I saw those wounded hands of yours, I guessed you were the young outlaw lad everyone's gossiping about. Ragi Haraldsson, isn't it? Don't try to deny it, my young friend. You're already infamous all over the islands!'

Ragi gulped the milk down. 'Then you've taken a huge risk helping me, haven't you?' he said awkwardly. 'I'd better leave straightaway, before anyone finds out. I can hide somewhere up on the moors. I wouldn't like you to...'

'No, no, stay put,' said Otkel firmly. 'I'm more than eager to help you. Guess why?'

Ragi shook his head.

Otkel winked. He pulled off his sealskin boots and rough, woollen socks. He wiggled his toes.

'You've got webbed feet like me!' cried Ragi in astonishment. 'But I thought... My uncles said...'

'Bit out of the ordinary, aren't we?' said Otkel. 'I've met one or two others like us here and there on the islands. We've all learned to keep quiet about it, but there's a secret kinship between us. Soon as I saw you were the same, I vowed to help you, and never mind the trouble you're in.'

'But it's really dangerous to help an outlaw!' said Ragi. 'I wouldn't want you to...'

'Danger's better than boredom,' said Otkel. 'But first, tell me the truth. Are these rumours going around true? You know, about that pedlar you were with?'

Ragi stiffened.

The laughter had drained from Otkel's voice. He said softly, 'People are saying he's that villain. *Him.* Grim Gruesome.' He paused. 'The child killer.'

He looked Ragi straight in the eye. 'And that you're in league with him. And that instead of making you an outlaw, Jarl Thorfinn should have killed you on the spot.'

Ragi's heart turned over as if Otkel had stabbed him. He tried to gather his thoughts together. He tried not to tremble. He tried to keep his voice steady.

'It's… The rumours are half true,' he admitted. 'It...it is Grim Gruesome. But I'm not in league with him. I swear I'm not! I swear by Thor! I swear by Odin All-Father and all the gods in Asgard! Please believe me, Otkel! I admit Grim Gruesome nearly persuaded me to join him – he's so cunning. But at the last minute, I changed my mind, I stood up to him, I swear I did. And that's why he…'

Otkel came and crouched beside the wall-bench.

'I believe you,' he said. 'But whatever is that brute up to? Why's he come here to Orkney?'

'He pretended he was after treasure...' said Ragi.

'Oh, did he now! What, from a *troll-mound*, I suppose?'

'Ya,' said Ragi. He gulped guiltily. 'He promised me treasure…to...to tempt me… He persuaded me to help him trap two girls…'

'Those girls from Tide Point!' cried Otkel at once. 'There's news of two girls missing from there. That's what got folks talking about Grim Gruesome.'

Ragi was in a sweat. He nodded.

'Grim Gruesome said we either had to go into this troll-mound ourselves, or trap other children and force *them* into it. I don't know if there's really a treasure inside it... But I do know that going into a mound means almost certain death!'

Otkel nodded bleakly.

'Grim Gruesome said that the trolls would kill them, and then he'd...*eat* them,' said Ragi.

'Odin's eye socket!' Otkel swore softly, shaking his ugly head.

'He's so cunning,' said Ragi. 'He trips you up and before you even realise what's happening, you're in his power. It was nine times worse than you could imagine, Otkel! Grim Gruesome... He's got this repulsive finger-stump... His threats make your blood freeze. He took the two girls away in his boat, to throw them to the trolls!'

'Shutting young girls into a troll-mound!' said Otkel. 'It doesn't bear thinking about! Farting giantesses, Ragi! The bravest warriors – berserks, even

– would rather die than go into one of those!'

'I know, I know,' said Ragi. 'Otkel, I've got to go after them and rescue them.' He thumped his forehead with his fist. 'It's all my stupid fault he caught them!'

'Good lad,' said Otkel. 'But try and calm down so you can tell me which mound he took them to. Which island is it on? There's not much in the way of mounds here on High Island... But somewhere on Mainland? Or on Hrolf's Island? There's some huge mounds out there.'

'When he first told me about the mound, he read out something from a rune-stone,' said Ragi. 'Aw, thunderbolts! I can't remember what it was. And...anyway, it's bound to be too late. They'll be dead already. Suffocated. Chopped up.' He shuddered again. '*Eaten...*'

'There might still be a chance,' said Otkel. 'Think, Ragi!'

Ragi closed his eyes. Grim Gruesome's peculiar, rasping voice was constantly echoing hauntingly through his mind. He thought back to their first meeting. He could still remember it clearly: Grim standing on the boat with the huge horse...the revolting finger-stump tracing the runes on the flat stone.

He said: 'It was something like, "...On a jagged island, Bare and cold, Stands a troll-mound, Full of gold."'

'Hmm,' said Otkel. 'I can think of loads of "jagged" islands, and most places in Orkney could be called "bare and cold". Is that all it said?'

'There was something else too…' said Ragi. '"Black Banks", I think. "South of the Black Banks", maybe.'

Otkel thought for a long moment. He tossed some more peats onto the fire, clouding the little room with smoke.

'I know these islands pretty well, Ragi,' he said. 'I know where most of the troll-mounds are too. But I've never heard of anywhere called Black Banks. I've no idea at all where this mound could be.'

27

Unn and Kadlin were squashed together inside the narrow, stone tunnel leading into the mound. It was too low even to sit up. It was impenetrably dark and chokingly stuffy. There was no escape.

They lay flat on their stomachs and shuffled along like worms. The tunnel floor was covered in sharp pebbles that tore their aprons and dresses, and scratched their legs.

After a short distance it opened out into what felt like a cave or a wide chamber. They stood up blindly, cautiously. There was just enough room not to bump their heads.

Kadlin was clutching the little strike-a-light box that Grim Gruesome had thrown in after them. She opened it with shaky hands and rubbed the fire-steel against the flint. When it sparked, she lit some touchwood from the box. Unn pushed the torch-stick into it and a flame flared up.

The air was so stale, the torch-stick burned only dimly. The two girls could just about see each other. They made out rough stone walls curving inwards to a low, domed ceiling. They gazed nervously at the shadows.

'How do you think the trolls get in?' whispered Unn.

'Not through that rock,' said Kadlin. 'It looked as if it hadn't been moved for hundreds of years. Perhaps they ooze up from under the ground?'

She shone the torch around. 'Or maybe there's another tunnel they use. Look: that might be one leading off on the right...and another one, opposite.'

'Freyja's tears!' trembled Unn. 'They're going to appear from all directions then. Oh Kadlin, they might jump on us at any moment!'

Kadlin squeezed her bigger cousin's hand. 'I've just thought,' she said. 'I've got a secret weapon, that might protect us from the trolls.'

'You?' said Unn. 'A weapon?'

'My ear-spoon,' said Kadlin proudly.

'Your *ear-spoon*?' said Unn. 'What good would that be? It's only a delicate little trinket…'

'It is not!' cried Kadlin. 'It's really useful. I clean my ears with it every single day. I've heard that all the noblewomen in Norway always carry them. You really ought to get one, Unn – your ears must be so dirty. Anyway, the point is, it's *metal*.'

'Huh?'

'Trolls and spooks are scared of metal,' said Kadlin.

'O…oh…ya!' cried Unn. 'You're right, I've heard people say that too… And we've got our shoulder-brooches as well… But hold on, they're all made of bronze. Isn't *iron* the only metal that scares trolls?'

Kadlin sighed. 'Aw, I think you're right. But what about the fire-steel? That's definitely made of iron. I'll hold it up to keep the trolls away. You shine the torch-stick around and look for the treasure.'

'I don't want to look,' quaked Unn. 'I don't want to see things jumping out at me!'

'Then…oh, let's swap,' said Kadlin impatiently. She thrust the fire-steel into her cousin's hand, snatched the torch-stick and crept deeper into the dark chamber…

'Aagh!'

'Thor's thunderbolts, what is it?' cried Unn.

'I just trod on something,' squealed Kadlin. 'It's…'

'What?'

'It felt like… I thought it was a piece of wood,' whispered Kadlin. 'But when I held the torch-stick over it, I saw… Oh, Unn, it's *bones*!'

'Bones?' said Unn. She swallowed loudly. 'You mean, animal bones?'

'No,' said Kadlin. 'Look!'

She felt for Unn's hand and pulled her closer, holding the torch-stick low to show up the floor. White against the sharp grey stones, lay a complete, child-sized, human skeleton.

28

'Goddess Freyja help us!' cried Unn. 'So it's true. The trolls really do kill people. And Grim Gruesome really eats them and chucks the bones back in here. Until I saw that, Kadlin, I'd hoped against hope...' she retched loudly. 'I'm going to be sick again.'

'Please don't!' said Kadlin. 'You'll stink the place out. Come on, we've got to try and find some treasure and get out of here as quickly as we can... Oh Unn, *now* look!'

'I'm too scared,' Unn whimpered. She held the firesteel high, covered her eyes with her other hand and shouted, 'We've got iron here, trolls! So just you keep away!' She dropped her voice. 'Oh Kadlin, I really can't stand any more of this.'

'But this is *gold*!' said Kadlin.

'Gold? REALLY? Where?' said Unn. In her confusion, she dropped the fire-steel, but suddenly she was too excited to notice. 'Quickly then, let's grab it all before the trolls come out, and take it straight to...you know, "him". And then maybe... Oh, please, mighty Thor, please, let him set us free!'

Kadlin squatted down, holding the torch carefully. Its flame lit up four shimmering golden discs.

Each one was slightly wider than their hands. Each was exquisitely engraved: circle within circle of mysterious patterns.

'Trolls' treasure!' breathed Unn.

'So beautiful!' cried Kadlin.

'Ya,' said Unn. 'But *weird*. I mean, what exactly are they? And those peculiar patterns... I've never seen anything like them before. Do you think we really dare take them? If the trolls catch us at it, they'll kill us.'

'They're going to kill us anyway, if we don't get out of here,' said Kadlin. 'And we haven't got a hope of doing that unless we take some treasure to Grim Gruesome.'

Unn squatted down, reached out to the nearest disc...and let out a shriek of horror: 'Oh no, I'm so clumsy!'

138

Under her fingers, the round edge of one disc had crumbled away.

'It must be trollish magic – making it turn invisible as soon as someone touches it,' said Kadlin. She moved the torch around. 'Oh! But it's all right. Look, it's just scattered all over the floor. Look how it sparkles in the torch flame! We should be able to pick most of it up. But be really careful, Unn, it's so thin, it must be very fragile.'

'Grim Gruesome will be furious with us for breaking it,' groaned Unn. 'And if it all goes like that when we touch it, how can we carry it out to him?'

'You can carry it in your apron,' said Kadlin at once. 'Mine's too flimsy.'

'But it'll all fall out as I crawl back.'

'No it won't,' said Kadlin. 'Because...look.'

She tugged at one of the tatty ribbons decorating her own apron and ripped it free. Then she carefully dropped some fragments of gold into Unn's apron and tied the edges together with the ribbon, making a neat bundle.

'You're brilliant!' said Unn.

'Let's gather it all up,' said Kadlin, 'and take it to Grim Gruesome straight away.'

Unn kneeled down with her apron spread right out. Nimbly, Kadlin scooped the broken bits and the other golden discs into it, and secured it with the ribbon. Then they stooped into the tunnel, blew out the torch and crawled back to the entrance rock.

A cobweb-thin crack of daylight shone down one side of it.

'Grim Gruesome!' Unn yelled through it. 'We've done what you said – we've brought you some trolls' treasure!'

They heard Haski whinnying in the distance. Unn shouted again, more loudly. Heavy boots came stomping towards them.

Grim's enormous, hairy hand appeared round the edge of the rock. The finger-stump throbbed like an evil slug. He wrenched the rock away, just far enough for them to see his dark figure looming against the bright daylight.

'Where is it?' he growled.

'Unn's got it in her apron, sir,' said Kadlin.

'Come here, Unn,' said Grim Gruesome. 'Give it to me.'

He moved the rock right aside. Unn climbed clumsily out, gasping in the fresh air. Kadlin made to follow her.

'Unless you've got some treasure too, you stay there!' Grim roared at her. He pushed the rock firmly back, blocking her way.

'Kadlin!' cried Unn.

'Let me out!' screamed Kadlin, muffled behind the rock.

'Please sir, let her out too,' begged Unn.

'Give me the treasure,' Grim Gruesome hissed.

Unn was shaking. She glanced back anxiously at the mound, then sat down on the grass. Very carefully, she unknotted the ribbon and unfolded the edges of her apron.

The sun broke thinly through dark clouds, eerily lighting up the heap of gold against the dirty folds of cloth.

Grim Gruesome took a step towards her. He stooped down and reached out. His smell was overpowering. Yellow bubbles of pus oozed from his finger-stump. He snatched up a handful of the gold and let it trickle back into her lap.

Unn stayed stock still.

Grim Gruesome strode across to Haski, who was grazing just a short way down the slope. He fiddled in his saddlebag and came back with a small box made of yellowish-white walrus ivory. He scraped the gold from her apron into the box.

When he was finished, Unn whispered, 'Please sir, you said…'

'Ya, you can go, Unn,' Grim Gruesome growled. 'I've finished with you.'

29

'Oh, thank you, sir!' said Unn. 'But… How will we get home? We don't even know where we are… Is there a village or harbour near here, where we can catch a ferry back to Tide Point?'

'No,' said Grim.

Unn's face fell. 'Oh! Then how ever…? And please don't forget Kadlin, sir, she's still shut in.'

Grim Gruesome didn't move.

Unn went back to the mound entrance and put her hands helplessly on the rock.

'Please sir,' she said, 'it's too heavy for me.'

'Leave it,' said Grim Gruesome.

'But Kadlin…'

'You go,' said Grim Gruesome. 'She stays.'

'But…'

'You brought me the trolls' treasure,' said Grim Gruesome. 'She brought me nothing.'

'That's not true!' cried Unn. 'We found it together.'

Grim Gruesome ignored her. 'You are free, but she stays a prisoner.'

'No!'

'You will grow up and live to tell the tale of your adventure,' growled Grim Gruesome. 'But Kadlin must wait in the suffocating darkness until the trolls tear her into blood-soaked pieces for me to devour. And their torments will be even more cruel than usual, because you have stolen their treasure.'

He smacked his lips noisily. 'Mmm! I can already imagine the delicious sound of her screams. She's so puny, the trolls will finish her off and chop her up for me in no time. Tender young girl-meat. My mouth is watering!'

'But I can't go and leave Kadlin in the troll-mound!' cried Unn. 'She's my best cousin – we do everything together – I love her! You can't let just one of us go free!'

'Can't I?' said Grim Gruesome. 'How will you make me change my mind?'

'By...by...by... Oh, it's not fair!' said Unn desperately.

'"Not fair!"' Grim Gruesome mocked her.

'You threw us in the mound together,' said Unn. 'We found the treasure together…'

'But only *you* gave it to me, Unn Sharp-Tongue,' said Grim Gruesome. 'You should have thought it through before you called me so urgently, you little fools.'

'Please!' begged Unn. All her impudence was gone. Tears streamed down her face. She dropped to her knees and held up her hands imploringly. '*Please*, sir, I beg you: let Kadlin go free too!'

'Hmm,' said Grim Gruesome. 'I've already shown you more mercy than I ought to, Unn. But I'm enjoying this game so much, I've just thought of an even better bargain. Ya, I'll set your cousin free and let her go home – and in return, you must join me and help me trap more children. I heard you discussing it on board my boat. You were quite keen on the idea then, weren't you?'

Unn stared at him in dismay.

'You know I can't do that,' she cried. 'And I can't go away and leave Kadlin here either. Whichever one I did, my family would be so ashamed, they'd disown me – just like Ragi's kinsfolk did. And if other people found out what I'd done, my whole family would be in disgrace. Jarl Thorfinn would probably kick them out of Orkney, and then poor Grandmam and Grandpa would die of shame.'

She closed her eyes and buried her face in her hands.

30

By the time Unn managed to wipe away her tears, Grim Gruesome had vanished. She gazed around in numb disbelief. Then she turned back to the mound.

The rock blocking the entrance was firmly wedged in place. But there was a thin fissure down the side of it where Grim Gruesome had prised it away with his sword.

'Kadlin?' she called into it. 'He's gone! Are you there? Are you all right?'

There was a long pause. Then Kadlin called back in a quivering voice, 'Not really. I heard everything he said. Oh, the evil brute!'

'I'm so sorry!' cried Unn. 'I tried my best...'

'Of course you did. It's not your fault,' said Kadlin generously. 'You'd better... You know, try to find your way home. There's no point in us both…' she gulped. '…dying.'

'Don't be stupid. Even if I knew how to get home, I'd never go without you,' said Unn. 'You know I wouldn't! Oh poor Kadlin, it must be twice as scary, shut up in there all on your own in the darkness.'

Kadlin didn't answer. But a muffled sob escaped through the crack.

'Anyway, how can we get home without even a boat?' said Unn. 'Thor help us! What are we going to do?'

In her frustration, she thumped the rock hard.

It wobbled.

'The rock's loose!' cried Unn. 'Oh, if only you were stronger, Kadlin – you might be able to push it free.'

Inside the mound she heard Kadlin shuffling about…then a loud grunt. Kadlin was trying to push with all her might against the rock. And it did shift, very, very slightly…then at once creaked back into place.

There was a long silence. Then Kadlin called out, 'I've just had an idea. I'm sure there are loads of stones lying around on the hill, aren't there? Listen, Unn: go and fetch as many of them as you can – both big ones and small ones.'

'Whatever for?'

'I'll explain when you've got them,' Kadlin urged her. 'Please. Hurry!'

Soon Unn had piled loads of different-sized stones next to the rock. Kadlin pushed the rock and managed to shift it again slightly.

'Quickly!' she yelled. 'Ram a small stone into the gap.'

It worked. Now the rock couldn't fall right back. Kadlin pushed a tiny bit more and Unn wedged in another, bigger stone. And so they went on.

It was incredibly hard work and it took them ages. But at last they had made an opening big enough for Unn to get her hands around, so she could pull as Kadlin pushed.

Gradually Unn built up an uneven pile of stones between the rock and the tunnel wall, leaving just enough room for Kadlin to squeeze through.

'I hope it doesn't slip back and crush you,' said Unn nervously.

'As you're much stronger than me,' said Kadlin, 'could you lean against it to keep it open?'

Unn stooped clumsily into the opening and put her weight against the rock, half inside the cave. Kadlin began to edge out…

'Oh no!' screamed Unn.

Her foot had blundered against the precarious pile of stones – and it had collapsed! The stones tumbled away down the slope. Unn teetered with a shriek...

The rock creaked free – and started crashing down towards her!

'Aagh! Help!'

Kadlin had no time to think. She did the only thing she could to save her cousin's life. She grabbed Unn's hand – and pulled her right inside the tunnel...just before the rock fell firmly back into place.

Now both the girls were trapped!

31

A biting wind whipped across the lonely grass and rocks below the troll-mound. Sea birds soared and screeched overhead.

Inside the mound, the darkness was thick as soup. The air was stuffy and stale.

Unn and Kadlin huddled in the cramped chamber, clinging to each other. They were weak with hunger, parched with thirst, too shrivelled up to cry. They dozed in and out of nightmares.

They couldn't stop thinking about the skeleton lying there, somewhere very close. The ground creaked. The walls hissed.

Time stretched. Time stopped.

Waiting for the nightmares to come true: that was the worst thing of all.

32

Thud. Thud.

Suddenly the girls jerked awake.

'Kadlin!' sobbed Unn. 'They're coming. Trolls!'

Thud. Rumble. Scrape.

They wrapped their arms tightly around each other. They held their breath.

'This is it: we're going to die!' said Unn.

'Where's that fire-steel?' Kadlin was hoarse with exhaustion. 'Iron might still save us…'

'I'm so sorry,' sobbed Unn. 'I dropped it…when we first found the gold.'

Kadlin cursed like an old sailor. Then she suddenly remembered: 'My needle-box! Some of the needles in it are made of iron…' She fumbled for a moment. 'Ya, it's still hanging from my brooch. Here – oh, quickly! – take one.'

'Ow, you've pricked me!'

'Just take it!' squealed Kadlin.

They held out the needles towards the noises.

'Keep away, you wicked trolls!' called Unn in a quavering voice. 'We've both got iron here!'

Thud. Creak.

A beam of daylight swept into the darkness, dazzling them.

'They must have opened the entrance rock!' gasped Unn.

'But trolls always hide from the light,' said Kadlin.

'Then – oh, mighty Thor! – it must be Grim Gruesome come back to finish us off!' wept Unn. 'Iron's no use against him.'

A shadow blocked the daylight. A strike-a-light flashed. There was a hissing noise. A torch-stick flared up in the tunnel and lit up a face.

33

'Freyja's tears!' cried Unn. 'That looks like the outlaw boy!'

'But we saw him drown!' cried Kadlin.

'Then – oh, Thor, I can't bear it!' sobbed Unn. 'It must be his *ghost*!'

Kadlin drew in her breath sharply. 'Ya, they say ghosts lurk in troll-mounds too.'

Unn's sobs turned into hysterical screams: 'No, NO!...'

'I'm not a ghost.' A voice echoed weirdly in the long passage. 'I didn't drown. It's really me, Ragi. Please don't be afraid. I won't hurt you, I swear it. I'm going to save you – even if I die doing it!'

They heard him grunting and swearing as he squeezed into the narrow opening. He was much taller and broader than the girls. But somehow he managed to wriggle awkwardly along the cramped tunnel, brandishing the flickering, smoking torch-stick in front of him.

The girls struggled to their feet and pressed themselves against the wall.

'Don't trust him,' whispered Unn. 'Remember, he tricked us before.'

'I don't know…' Kadlin hissed back. 'Maybe…'

'I didn't want to trap you!' cried Ragi. 'You've seen how Grim Gruesome forces people to do things. I swear by Thor and Odin and all the gods in Asgard – I'm truly sorry for what I did and for everything that happened.'

'Liar!' screeched Unn. 'I bet Grim Gruesome saved you somehow – and sent you here. How else could you have found us?'

Ragi didn't answer. He emerged from the tunnel and stood up in the chamber, bumping his head on the stone ceiling.

'Believe me!' he begged. 'I've come to save you. Why else would I be here? I hate Grim Gruesome as much as you do. I feel so ashamed of everything he made me do.'

Air rushed in through the opening behind him, making his torch burn more brightly, lighting up the trollish prison.

The girls clutched each other and gazed around, wide-eyed. They saw walls built of huge, rough-cut boulders, and gravel on the floor. Two side-rooms led from the main chamber. In the darkness they had stumbled into one of these… And without realising it, had been lying almost on top of another skeleton!

'Aagh!' screamed Unn. She jerked away from it. 'Freyja's tears, outlaw boy! How many people have you and Grim Gruesome thrown to the trolls before us?'

'None, I tell you!' shouted Ragi.

But Kadlin interrupted him with a cry. 'Oh! Just look at *that*.'

Behind the second skeleton, something was gleaming. More treasure – much more!

A big heap of finger-sized half-rings, their open ends shaped like drooping flowers; several bracelets, each as wide as a hand, roughly engraved with mysterious patterns; thick, twisted neck-bands; a large, quarter-moon shaped ornament with a circle at either end. All so crudely made. But not fragile like the discs they'd found before: these were solid, heavy gold.

'It's so weird!' breathed Unn.

Kadlin nodded. 'Definitely the work of trolls.'

Ragi let out a long whistle. 'Let's share it. You two gather it up - then get yourselves out of here.'

Kadlin coaxed Unn onto the floor. They scrabbled up the treasures into their aprons, securing them with Kadlin's ribbons. Ragi clambered back over the skeleton and moved the torch around.

'I'll be with you in a moment. I just want to see what's in the other chamber, across there.'

He stooped under the sloping roof to explore it.

'There's a bit more treasure...' he called. 'No, not treasure... This is a *sword*. Oh wow! Just what I need in case... Quickly, you two get the gold out. I'll bring this.'

Aprons overflowing, Kadlin and Unn crawled down the tunnel and squeezed out of the entrance hole. They dropped their hoard onto the grass and gulped in great mouthfuls of fresh air, crying with relief.

The sky was dark with glowering storm clouds and the wind was fierce.

Ragi followed them out, dragging the troll-sword.

His hands were still red and swollen, horribly like Grim Gruesome's scars.

Unn recoiled from him.

But Kadlin whispered, 'I think we should trust him. He could have harmed us, but he didn't.'

'But how can we be sure?' Unn hissed back.

'He got us out of there safely, that's how!' said Kadlin.

Ragi laid the sword carefully on the grass and faced them, smiling sheepishly. 'So this is what the trolls would have used to slice you up for Grim Gruesome,' he said.

'Goddess Freyja's amber tears!' shrieked Unn.

The sword was a truly unearthly weapon, nothing like the Vikings' iron swords. It had a gold-like sheen, no crossbar and a strangely curved blade: narrow near the top, broadening to a wide, razor-sharp tip.

Unn shivered. 'Those skeletons…'

'They must be other children that Grim Gruesome lured here,' said Ragi.

'Shut up!' shrieked Unn.

They didn't waste any more time, but made their way, stumbling and slipping, down a heather-covered slope. At the bottom was another fjord, with a small rowing boat moored there.

'That's not Grim Gruesome's boat,' said Kadlin.

'No,' said Ragi. 'It's mine. Well, not exactly mine...I had a bit of an adventure getting here. I borrowed this from a village nearby. Never mind, just get in.'

They climbed aboard and laid the trolls' treasure very carefully in the bottom with the mysterious sword beside it. Ragi took up a pair of oars and pulled away from the shore.

Thunder rumbled across the sky. The storm clouds broke into torrential rain, lit by a dazzle of lightening.

In no time, they were all drenched. But the girls hardly cared. They turned up their faces to catch the raindrops in their parched mouths.

So they didn't see another boat that suddenly appeared from the open sea, heading straight towards them.

But Ragi did. 'Aw no! Farting giantesses!' he yelled.

In the other boat stood a huge horse. And the massive, glowering figure of Grim Gruesome.

34

'WHAT?' Grim Gruesome's roar rang out against the noise of the stormy sea. 'You cunning maggot, Unn Sharp-Tongue! How did you drag your cousin from the mound? I was on my way to check the trolls had finished slaughtering her and to guzzle the flesh from her bones! And you, Ragi Haraldsson – I saw you drown. Odin's eye socket! How dare you come swanking back from the dead?'

Ragi gritted his teeth. He clutched the oars bravely in his swollen hands and kept rowing. Unn and Kadlin grabbed an oar each, and helped him feebly. They reached the place where the little fjord opened out to the sea.

Grim Gruesome suddenly swept his boat in front of them. He turned it sideways, blocking the opening.

There was no way round him!

Frantically, Ragi tried to steer past. But Grim Gruesome zigzagged in their way, then back again. He steered his boat at theirs, forcing them towards the shore.

Ragi dropped his oars and grabbed the troll sword.

Across the water, Haski whinnied. Grim Gruesome reached under his cloak and pulled out his own sword. Then he leaped into the sea. He was monstrously tall. He came splashing towards them with giant-like strides.

Ragi jumped into the water too.

'Keep rowing!' he yelled at the girls. He gave their boat a hard shove. 'Go on, get away while you can!'

He ran nimbly through the waves to the beach. Grim Gruesome waded after him.

Unn grabbed the tiller and tried to swing the boat round towards the open sea.

'No, wait!' Kadlin begged her. 'We can't just... He saved us from the mound, Unn! We're all in this together now. We've got to help him.'

'Don't be stupid,' snorted Unn. 'He's a boy and he's got a sword. If he can't beat Grim Gruesome, what use are we?'

'We've got to try,' Kadlin insisted. She was already clambering out of the boat and paddling through the shallows.

'Come back!' Unn screamed at her. 'You're so delicate, you'll be hurt in no time. You'll spoil...'

But Kadlin was running up the short beach onto the grass.

Unn stared after her in despair. She put down her oar uncertainly and bit her lip. She dabbed her eyes. Then with a sigh, she too clambered out and lumbered after her cousin.

Ahead of them, Grim Gruesome and Ragi were already fighting. Metal clanged and clashed. Unn screamed as she saw Grim's enormous, bloodstained sword coming down on Ragi's neck!

But Ragi ducked and dodged it. He raced up the slope. Grim Gruesome, grunting like an angry boar, strode after him. Foul black spittle dribbled down his mufflers.

The troll-mound stood at the top, its entrance gaping open. Grim leaped at Ragi, knocked the troll-sword from the boy's grasp and forced him towards it. Ragi struggled wildly.

Grim Gruesome held up his left hand and waved

his repulsive finger-stump before Ragi's eyes. To and fro it went, to and fro, stinking of festering pus.

Ragi screwed his eyes tight shut. Grim Gruesome poked them open with his hairy thumb, and thrust his throbbing stump before them again.

Slowly, the colour drained from Ragi's face. He began to sway...

The girls had almost caught up with them. They scurried round the mound and huddled behind it.

'We need to distract him...' whispered Kadlin. 'Give Ragi a chance to...'

'I can't, I can't. I'm too scared!' Unn whimpered.

Kadlin huffed furiously – grabbed Unn's hand – and pulled her from their hiding place.

'No!' shrieked Unn.

But Grim Gruesome had seen them. He hissed like a snake.

Ragi was slumping to the ground. Grim Gruesome turned and lunged at the girls. He grabbed Kadlin with his deformed hand. He lifted her up and spun her round. Then he strode off, carrying her towards the cliff. Below it, a deep chasm fell away through the rocks to the churning sea.

'Let her go!' screamed Unn. She stumbled after them. 'Oh, Kadlin, my darling cousin...I warned you not to...'

Ragi sat up shakily and blinked. He took in what was happening. He saw the troll-sword. He forced himself to his feet and ran across to seize it.

Somehow, Unn caught up with Grim Gruesome. For a long moment she hesitated. But now she was in the thick of it, now it was life or death, she found her courage at last. She leaned forward – grabbed hold of Kadlin's legs – and held on fast, tugging against Grim Gruesome with all her might.

Grim Gruesome began to snort and cough.

'Help!' Kadlin screamed. 'I'm tangled up in him!'

A string of her glass beads was caught fast in an animal claw that hung from one of Grim Gruesome's fur mufflers. As Unn battled to drag her away, the fur pulled tighter and tighter against the brute's neck. Grim tried to loosen it with his free hand. But the more he fiddled, the tighter it got. He yanked it still harder...

And suddenly the string of beads came loose. One end smashed up hard into the shadows where Grim

Gruesome's face was hidden. His head jerked back with a spine-chilling yelp. He dropped Kadlin – and raised his enormous boot. He was going to trample her! But no, his foot missed its mark and thudded clumsily onto the ground...

'GRIM GRUESOME!' Ragi yelled. He raced past the brute, towards the edge of the cliff. Grim Gruesome staggered after him. Ragi spun round and lunged at Grim with the troll-sword.

Grim Gruesome struck back at once. But he was way off target: his sword sliced through empty air. The beads must have hit him in the eye! He teetered blindly above the chasm. His great arms spun madly, clutching at emptiness...

He toppled over!

There was a long moment of silence. Then an almighty SPLASH! as he hit the deep, dark water.

35

The three children ran as fast as they could down the slope and back to the beach. The ebbing tide had carried Ragi's boat out into the fjord. But he swam easily after it, jumped in and rowed back to fetch the girls.

They each took an oar – even puny Kadlin – and soon reached the sea-opening. But Grim Gruesome's boat still blocked their way, for Haski was stamping angrily up and down in it, making it dart about, this way, that way, backwards and forwards.

'After all this, now we still can't get out of here!' sobbed Unn.

All at once, the waves seemed to drag backwards. The water smoothed briefly, then began to churn about again as a stream of bubbles gurgled to the surface.

Grim Gruesome's boat was swept towards the cliff. Haski whinnied in alarm.

The children rowed past with all their might. They rounded the headland and turned onto the open sea.

They didn't look back. They didn't see a circle of dark, round heads with long whiskers pop up. The heads stared after them unblinkingly for a long moment. Then they sank silently and vanished.

36

Ragi had a stale loaf of flat bread in the boat and the children all gobbled it down greedily. But before long, Unn was violently seasick again. Ragi rowed on, keeping as near to the coast as possible. Kadlin did her utmost to help him, biting her lip as she strained on her oar, fighting the storm with all her feeble strength. The land they passed was as wild as ever, with not a single house in sight.

Night fell briefly. Dawn broke.

The gale blew up again. This time it brought rain, pelting down as if the gods themselves were emptying buckets from the sky. The sea heaved. Waves surged into the boat, mixing with the rain into a deep, swirling puddle.

Poor Unn was white as ice. She kneeled against the

side of the boat, gagging and moaning. But even so she did what she could, scooping water in her shaking hands and flinging it out over the side.

A huge wave washed right over them. Ragi and Kadlin dropped the oars and frantically baled alongside Unn. Still the rain beat down, stinging like whips.

'Dwarf spit!' swore Ragi. 'The coastline's vanished. Where are we?'

'Lost!' wept Unn.

In every direction there was nothing but rain and sea. The boat rocked and dipped and spun around.

'Look!' shrieked Kadlin suddenly. She pointed. 'Ships!'

A wavering grey line seemed to separate the churning sea from the thunderous sky. Just before it, they saw the silhouettes of three longships with square sails, tossing on the waves.

Ragi screwed up his eyes. 'They've got their sails up...they're moving. They look as if they're still in control, heading somewhere...'

'That dark thing behind them,' said Kadlin. 'Is it land?'

'Please let's try and reach them,' begged Unn. 'Surely they'll help us?'

The sea decided for them. A fast undercurrent was already carrying their boat towards the ships.

Ragi yanked hard on the tiller. Slowly the boat turned until it was directly facing the longships. Kadlin carried on baling urgently. In-between vomiting, Unn helped as much as she could. Ragi started rowing again.

The storm raged. They saw monstrous shapes pass darkly through the waves and sky: whale fins, shark fins, shrieking birds with huge wingspans. In the bottom of the boat, the strange golden treasure slopped about, gleaming under its covering of storm water.

Soon they could make out the three ships quite clearly. They were huge war-ships, each with a row of round shields clipped along the sides. Their beautiful, swan-curved prows showed their owner must be both rich and powerful. Their brightly coloured sails billowed in the gale. Men swarmed on their decks. There was a rhythmic splashing as dozens of oars rose and fell in unison. And Kadlin was right: behind the ships loomed a dark island.

But it was high and completely sheer. There was no place to land.

The ships' crews had seen them. Now one of the

vessels turned and headed towards them.

'Oh please, mighty Thor!' groaned Unn. 'Please let them rescue us!'

The ship was almost upon them, gracefully riding the churning waves. The helmsman held up his hand in greeting and called: 'Stay where you are. We'll try and take you aboard.'

Slowly the ship drew alongside them.

'Odin's eye socket!' the helmsman shouted to his crew. 'There's just a bunch of children in this boat – and two of them girls!'

Then to the children he called, 'Hold tight! We'll throw you some ropes.'

Two coils of thick rope came spinning through the air. They fell in the sea and were thrown again. This time, Ragi caught one and the other landed on the floor of the boat. He tied them round the girls' waists.

'Now jump!' the helmsman shouted.

The churning waves were dark and white-frothed, roaring with the threat of watery death.

'I can't, I can't!' screamed Unn.

Ragi dragged her to the side, lifted her up, threw her towards the ship...

She missed it and fell heavily into the deep water. It

seemed to swallow her... But she bobbed up again, was dragged swiftly through the waves and hauled onto the broad deck. The rain still pelted down, but strong arms grasped her and laid her gently in the shelter of a barrel.

Kadlin followed in the same way, but more willingly.

'Now you, lad!' yelled the helmsman.

Ragi shook his head. 'I'm not leaving the boat,' he called. 'It's full of treasure!'

Several of the oarsmen leaned over, straining to see. Ragi stood astride the rowing bench, rocking up and down.

'Silver?' a man called.

'Gold!' Ragi answered.

'Odin's eye socket!' cried the helmsman again. 'Where did you find a hoard like that round these wild parts?'

'In a mound,' Ragi answered. 'It's *trolls'* treasure!'

A shout went up from the crew and the helmsman blew loudly on a horn. Through the storm, Ragi saw the lead ship slowly turning round in the swell and rowing back towards them.

Now the two ships were next to each other. Men

shouted. The helmsman of the lead ship climbed up onto its sidewall. He stood tall and lean in the storm, with long, athletic legs, measuring the swell with his eye. Then suddenly he made a leap across to the other ship.

But at that very moment, a great wave came crashing up. It forced the two vessels wide apart – too late for the lead helmsman to stop. For a frozen moment, his arms flailed wildly and his feet thrashed through the empty air. Then he went crashing into the sea.

And at once a cry rang out through the storm: 'All hands here! Jarl Thorfinn's gone overboard – he's near drowning!'

37

Several men jumped into the water after the Jarl. Others threw ropes. The rest heaved at the oars, trying to shelter the Jarl with the three ships. But none of this was enough to overcome the violence of the storm. It tossed the ships around like twigs and forced the men back.

As for the Jarl: one minute he was swimming powerfully and reaching for a rope...and the next he was being tossed away by the waves!

Ragi stared after him in horror. *This sea's a puking death trap!* he thought. *First it got Grim Gruesome and now the Jarl!* Then relief flooded him. *But they're both my enemies. The sea must be on my side!*

He heard a shout and turned. Now the Jarl was

floundering close behind his boat.

Ragi scowled down at the man who had condemned him to such pain and hunger, and gloated.

Two brawny men were trying to swim towards the Jarl, but the seething torrents kept driving them apart.

Huh! thought Ragi. *I can swim better than them. I could easily save him.*

He rubbed his swollen hands together. All the rowing and sword-fighting had made them raw and tender again, bringing back dark, resentful memories of the Ordeal Test. He watched the Jarl thrashing and struggling in the churning water.

But why should I, after what he did to me?

The Jarl's head turned towards him. For a brief moment their eyes met. *That was me a few days ago,* Ragi thought. *Dwarf spit! I'll never forget feeling that I was about to die!* A chill shuddered down his spine. *But someone – or something – saved me then. So if I had any honour...* He swallowed. *...I suppose...I'd put the past behind me and do the same for him.*

He hesitated a moment longer...then dived in.

The water was freezing, but it held him safe. He rode the swell, steadying himself, letting it flow through his bare, webbed feet. The Jarl's men were still thrashing about uselessly. Swiftly, smoothly, Ragi crossed the short distance to Jarl Thorfinn.

'Here, sir!' he yelled.

He reached out. The Jarl was weakening, slipping below the surface, barely staying afloat. His huge hand inched towards Ragi.

Ragi caught it, eased himself alongside and pushed his own sore hands under the great man's armpits. He twisted round onto his back, paddling with his feet, and dragged the Jarl through the waves. They reached the boat. Ragi clambered aboard and helped Jarl Thorfinn up after him.

For a few moments the Jarl just sprawled over the sodden rowing benches, gasping heavily and spitting out sea-water. Then he sat up and his eye fell on the golden treasure.

'By all the gods in Asgard,' he cried. 'Where did you get hold of this extraordinary stuff?'

He seized the golden quarter-moon ornament and examined it carefully. Then he stared hard at Ragi, narrowing his piercing blue eyes.

'You! I know who you are. You're the lad I outlawed less than half a month ago!'

Ragi nodded.

'And even then you dared to commit another despicable crime,' said the Jarl. 'You abducted the granddaughters of the old fisherman at Tide Point who used to supply me with lobsters. '

'I never did!' protested Ragi. 'I've just rescued them from…'

Jarl Thorfinn shook his head. He squeezed the water from his beard. 'There are rumours that you are in league with that brute Grim Gruesome,' he said. 'I should kill you on the spot. But you're obviously not drownable. And my sword seems to have floated away in this farting sea. Anyway, I *can't* kill you. Not when you've just saved my life. For even I, Jarl of all this realm, must bow to Odin's law that a gift must be returned.'

Ragi met his gaze.

The Jarl smiled thinly. 'You're lucky, Ragi Haraldsson. You gave me my life. So I must give you yours in exchange.'

38

The sea had swept them to a lonely island almost beyond the western horizon. When the storm finally died, the Jarl's men took their master aboard the lead ship. Then Ragi rowed after the battered and bedraggled fleet, round the rocky coastline to a small harbour full of diving, shrieking seagulls. A single stone farmhouse with a turf roof stood above it.

The farmer's wife didn't bat an eyelid when she saw 150 men – including Jarl Thorfinn Skull-Splitter himself! – and three children coming ashore. She was well used to dealing with shipwrecks.

Her house was lined with plain timbers and simply furnished, but there was plenty of room in it. The good woman stoked up the peat fire and set an enormous cauldron of beef stew to cook on it. Meanwhile, her five daughters went outside to their beer barrel, filled buckets from it and passed these around the throng with drinking horns and wooden cups. By the time the farmer himself came home, his house was full of cheer with a tasty feast laid out in honour of their noble guest.

Kadlin and Unn soon came round in the warmth and ate a hearty meal. Then Jarl Thorfinn called them to stand before him and tell him everything that had happened, and especially Ragi's role in it.

The Jarl was a hard and worldly man, but even he looked astonished when the girls explained how the pedlar had tricked all three of them – and then revealed himself to be the evil Grim Gruesome. He listened carefully as they told how Ragi had rescued them from the troll-mound, and how they had all battled against the villain. He nodded somberly as they described Grim Gruesome's fall to his death.

'Please sir,' said Unn when they'd finished, 'can I ask Ragi some questions?'

'You may indeed,' said the Jarl.

'I've been puzzling this over and over,' said Unn. 'How on earth did you survive drowning? And how did you find us?'

So Ragi told how Otkel Mushroom-Nose had rescued him from the sea, and their discussion about the strange 'treasure' message on Grim Gruesome's rune-stone.

'At first Otkel couldn't think where this "jagged island south of Black Banks" might be,' he said. 'But he kept saying that it sounded familiar – and then he suddenly realised that it isn't in Orkney at all. It's a narrow stretch of sea in the islands of *Shetland*.'

'Oh!' exclaimed Kadlin. 'So that's where we are! Fancy us travelling all the way to Shetland!'

'The most northerly part of my realm,' said Jarl Thorfinn. 'And this welcoming little place here is on its western edge. It's called Bird Island. But go on, Ragi. How did you get there?'

'My hands were starting to heal from the Ordeal Test,' said Ragi, 'but they were still too sore to row all that way. Otkel can't row any distance either, because he's too disabled with his humpback. And he didn't dare ask anyone else to help, because everyone had already heard about me being made an outlaw. But that evening, some neighbours called by and said they were sailing up to Muddy Bay in Shetland to deliver some goods, and did Otkel want anything taken up

180

there? So he hid me in a barrel, pretended it was full of his home-brewed beer, and asked them to deliver that.'

The Jarl was watching Ragi intently. 'Go on.'

'They never guessed I was hiding inside,' said Ragi. 'At Muddy Bay, they dumped the barrel outside the drinking hall. Once the coast was clear, I sneaked out and asked around how to get to Black Banks. Luckily, no one guessed I was an outlaw. An old fellow told me to ride west then north, then west, then north again, to a village at the head of a fjord, and then to continue north-west on the sea. So when it finally got dark, I stole a horse from a field... I'm sorry, about that, sir, but you understand now that this was really urgent?'

'I'd have done exactly the same in your position,' the Jarl nodded.

'...And rode through the night to this village. There I borrowed...well, stole...a boat and rowed out of the fjord. It didn't take me long to find an island that looked "jagged". And when I circled it, I easily spotted the troll-mound on top of a hill. But I was really worried that Grim Gruesome might have already killed the girls and...' he swallowed. 'You know... devoured them.'

'He would have done, if a gale hadn't blown Grim

Gruesome's boat right off course on the way there,' said Kadlin.

'I felt sure I was almost dead when you broke into the mound,' said Unn. 'I'll never forget how you saved us, Ragi. I'm going to tell everyone what a hero you are!'

Ragi turned bright red. But secretly his heart gave a little leap of pride.

A smile spread across Jarl Thorfinn's severe face. 'This is a truly extraordinary adventure,' he said. 'The poets and story makers will surely weave it into a most marvellous legend! Meanwhile, I must decide what to do with you.'

Ragi raised his head. He looked the Jarl frankly in the eye.

'You've already given up your right to kill me,' he said. 'I don't expect any more favours from you. But please, sir, now I have the trolls' treasure, may I pay a fine and buy my freedom?'

'No,' said the Jarl.

Ragi looked devastated.

But the Jarl went on: 'You have done three great deeds: You have saved my life. You have saved the lives of these two girls. And you have rid my realm of an evil villain. In return, from this moment I, Thorfinn Turf-Einarsson the Skull-Splitter, Jarl of all the islands that lie north and west of Britain, release you from being an outlaw.

'There is no need to pay. You have won back your freedom for ever, Ragi Haraldsson. And in recognition of your heroism, from now on you shall carry a new name.'

He turned to the throng.

'Listen, people!' he cried. 'This boy has defied trolls and destroyed Grim Gruesome. So let him be known throughout my realm as Ragi Monster-Slayer!'

39

After the storm died down, fresh ships were sent to Bird Island to replace the ones that had been wrecked. They carried Ragi, Kadlin and Unn back to Orkney with Jarl Thorfinn Skull-Splitter and his noblemen.

When they arrived at Fortress Island, the Jarl split the bag of golden trolls' treasure between them, so that each child had an equal share.

He sent the girls back to Tide Point with a special escort. And he gave Ragi a wonderful gift: his very own horse! You can imagine how proud Ragi felt, riding home on it so grandly, with his bag of treasure on the saddle beside him.

He felt better still when he arrived and all the other lads came crowding round, admiring the horse and offering their congratulations. For gossip of his adventure had travelled ahead of him and already everyone knew that he was now a great hero. No one sneered at him any more. Instead, everyone was eager to be his friend.

But the best thing of all happened when he reached his little cottage.

Laughter was drifting out through the open door. A *man's* laughter. This was very odd, because his mother Alfdis had kept away from men ever since Ragi's father had died.

He went in cautiously – and nearly fainted in astonishment. There, sitting opposite his mother before a roaring fire, was none other than Otkel Mushroom-Nose!

'Mam,' said Ragi awkwardly, 'I'm back. Jarl Thorfinn's pardoned me. I'm free!'

Widow Alfdis jumped up, flung her arms round Ragi and burst into tears of joy. 'I know, I know,' she wept. 'We already heard the news. My wonderful, brave boy…'

Ragi shrugged her off, biting his lip. 'But Otkel,' he said, 'what are *you* doing here?'

Otkel cracked his grotesque face into a broad grin. 'Well,' he said, ' I kept thinking about your poor mam out here. I guessed she must be worrying herself sick about what had happened to you. So I tidied myself up as well as I could and came over to reassure her that you were still alive. Luckily, she didn't faint with horror when she saw my ugly mutt!'

'Of course I didn't,' said Alfdis indignantly. 'As soon as Otkel told me how he'd helped you, I knew he was a good man.' She stepped back from Ragi and wiped away her tears on a corner of her apron. 'He was very sympathetic about your pa dying and the family throwing us out. In return, I invited him to stay for a meal. But you know how bad my cooking is...'

'So I ended up cooking it for her!' chuckled Otkel.

'And it was delicious,' said Alfdis. 'So in return for that, I said I'd sing for him...'

'And when I heard her lovely voice,' grinned Otkel. 'I couldn't resist taking out my pipes to accompany her...'

He patted the pan pipes dangling from his belt.

'...And we found that we both know exactly the same tunes,' said Alfdis.

Ragi stared from his mother to kindly Otkel, and back again. *Farting giantesses!* he thought. *This is embarrassing!*

'Anyway,' said Alfdis, 'the long and the short of it is, that we've decided to get married. What do you think of that?'

Ragi felt dizzy. After all the unspeakable things that had happened! He felt his heart would burst with happiness.

Otkel winked at him. Now that Ragi was used to him, he hardly noticed Otkel's humpback, or his squashed nose.

'I'll be like a father to you,' said Otkel. 'And you'll be like a son to me.' He pulled off his boots and wriggled his toes comically. 'How can it be any different, Ragi, when both of us have flipper-feet!'

40

The wedding took place at the end of the month. Thanks to Ragi's treasure, it was a very grand affair.

Of course, Kadlin and Unn were guests of honour: after what they'd been through together, Ragi said that he felt almost as if they were his sisters. Their grandparents had both changed their opinion of Ragi, and when Grandpa brought the girls to the wedding, he slapped Ragi's back in a very friendly way.

Alfdis even invited the kinsfolk who had so cruelly thrown her and Ragi off their farm, as well as all the local people who used to mock and taunt them. Because as Otkel pointed out, enemies just give you trouble. But if you turn them into friends, that's even better than being rich.

Jarl Thorfinn Skull-Splitter himself sent them a

magnificent wedding present: a great, black bear fur all the way from the frozen lands of the far north.

He also sent one of his own poets to the wedding, to recite the heroic tale of how Ragi Monster-Slayer had overcome a tribe of trolls and the villainous Grim Gruesome in a single adventure. The poet didn't forget to weave the bravery of Unn and Kadlin into the story too. So everyone ended up really happy.

But they might not have been so cheerful if they had realised that Grim Gruesome hadn't really died when he fell down that chasm to the sea.

For it seems that his monstrous strength kept the water out of his lungs, and that he somehow dragged himself up from the depths and swam back to his boat where Haski stood patiently waiting. He was never seen in any of the Jarl's islands again. But before long he was rumoured to be stalking other parts of the North Lands.

People unlucky enough to encounter him whispered that he had become more gruesome than ever. His rotten finger-stump, his burn-blistered arms and his poison-black saliva were all bad enough. But now, people said, if you peered up into his hood, you might glimpse one of his eyeballs hanging on a thread from its socket, where he had been hit by Kadlin's broken string of beads.

Of course, that just made the old villain hate children more than ever. No doubt you'd love to know how he got his revenge. But you'll have to wait – because that's another very grim and gruesome story!

'Wolf-guts! Whale-doom! This I swear:
I'll stalk vile children everywhere.
I'll snatch and spike them in my snare
and boil their bones in dark despair!'

Jarl Thorfinn Turf-Einarsson the Skull-Splitter was a real Viking jarl (earl) who lived in the 10th Century. His realm included the islands of Orkney and Shetland to the north, and the Hebrides to the west of Scotland.

Folklore in these islands is rich with ancient tales of the mysterious mounds which can still be seen there today; and of people with 'webbed' fingers or feet, rumoured to have a mystical relationship with the seals which abound in the local waters.

All the historical descriptions in the book are as accurate as possible, including Ragi's 'crime' of reciting poetry to a girl, his trial through an ordeal test and his punishment of being made an outlaw.

Visit the official Grim Gruesome website,

www.grimgruesome.com

to find out lots more about the books

and the historical background,

and to download some

fun Grim Gruesome themed activities.

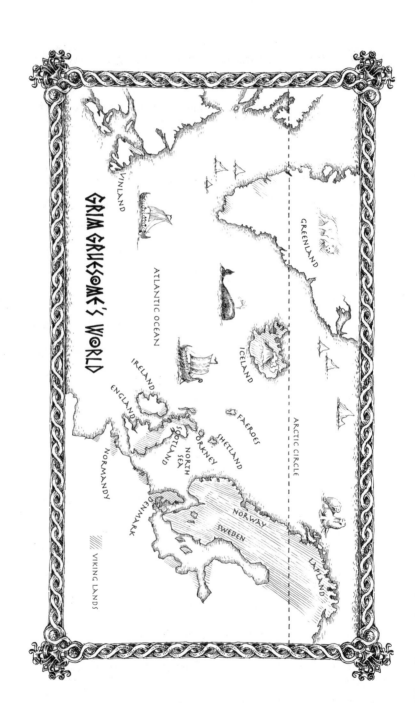